Twice as Sexy

Sexy Series Book #2
Club TEN29

CARLY PHILLIPS

He's the bad boy her mother warned her about.

The guy who makes her crave all the naughty things a good girl shouldn't want.

Tanner Grayson is a man outrunning the demons of his past and has the rap sheet to prove it. The only thing keeping old anger in check and him on the straight and narrow are the men he calls brothers and the club he calls home. He has no business taking the sexy woman doing shots in his club upstairs to his bed.

They never should have crossed paths. But when Assistant District Attorney Scarlett Davis lays eyes on the hot as sin club owner, she decides he's the birthday present she wants to unwrap at the end of the evening.

He tells himself it's one night. She convinces herself she deserves a short break from her latest case. But one night isn't enough and soon these two opposites are in deeper than they ever planned.

When Scarlett's case collides with Tanner's past, she sees the dangerous man he's hidden beneath the cool veneer he presents to the world. Can she accept him for who he is? Or will she run from the bad boy who makes her feel so good?

Chapter One

S CARLETT DAVIS SPENT too much time in her little corner of the district attorney's office not to personalize it and give the place some warmth. But not even the pretty succulent owl planters her best friend had bought for her birthday could make the dingy beige walls and linoleum floors bright and cheery. Still, she did her best to decorate and make her area feel like home. Even if her work was too important to worry about little things like atmosphere, she did what she could to brighten up her assigned space.

"Happy birthday to you. Happy birthday to you. Happy birthday, dear Scarlett, you'd better come out and celebrate with me or I'll cry boo-hoo," her best friend and fellow assistant district attorney, Leigh Michaels, sang as she entered Scarlett's office.

Scarlett shook her head and laughed at the pathetic attempt at a song. "That doesn't rhyme, just so you know, but thank you for the birthday wishes. And the present. I love them," she said, pointing to the owls she'd set out on the windowsill.

"You're welcome." The pretty brunette settled into the chair across from Scarlett's desk, a metal piece of furniture that was identical to every other one in the office. "So? We're going out tonight, right?"

With a sigh, Scarlett shook her head. "I can't, Leigh. You know how much work these cases I'm assigned have been. Just because we secured one conviction doesn't mean the other two are guaranteed."

Scarlett was second chair in a series of high-profile New York Mafia cases. She'd been inundated with work for the last year as each one came closer to their trial date. Picking up a pen, she began rolling it between her hands.

"You need a break," Leigh argued. "For all the work you've done and the way you've handled things, these might as well be *your* cases. Instead Kyle Morgan stands up and takes all the credit when everyone knows it's your smarts and instincts that have won these victories." She lowered her voice as she spoke, not wanting to get caught bad-mouthing someone higher up on the totem pole than she was.

"It is what it is. I don't need the credit, just the convictions." Scarlett lived for putting the bad guys away. It was the reason she'd studied criminal justice and had gone into law. The basis for why she'd chosen prosecution over defense as a career. She had a distinct

Twice as Sexy

disdain for people who committed crimes and got away with them and made it her mission to prevent those kinds of occurrences from happening.

She glanced at the photo of Hank, her younger brother, forever immortalized at sixteen years old, sitting on her desk. The picture never let her forget the reasons for her dedication to her work. Neither did the bracelet she wore that he'd given her when she turned eighteen. He'd worked at the corner grocery store and bought her what he could afford. A thin chain with a heart and she never took it off.

Leigh nodded. "And I respect that. But you only turn thirty once, and I have a connection that can get us into Club TEN29 tonight." She dropped the name as if it was an incentive to get Scarlett to change her mind about going out.

"I've never heard of the place."

At the admission, Leigh rolled her eyes. "Of course you haven't because all you do is work. If you picked your head up out of those files once in a while, you'd know it's the hot club in the city and we're lucky to get our names on a list to get in. They have live entertainment. Did you know they had a grand reopening with Lola Corbin and Charlotte Jasper?" She waggled her eyebrows at the mention of the well-known, popular rock stars.

Even Scarlett, who buried her head in work, knew

of them both and was impressed.

"And the club is not the same old watering holes the stuffy people around this office go to," Leigh said, continuing to push. "We could go out, let loose. Come on, you deserve it!"

Scarlett smiled at her persistent friend. "Fine. You're not going to let this go, so I might as well give in." She placed her pen down on the desk.

"Yay! I just happen to have an extra skirt and top in my bag for you to wear."

"Naturally," Scarlett muttered.

Leigh was nothing if not always prepared. She'd probably come to work today with this plan already in mind, knowing if she'd asked Scarlett in advance she'd have said no.

"Well, you're not going out looking like a prudish schoolmarm from another century," Leigh said with a disdain-filled glance at Scarlett's black pencil skirt and matching silk top. Her striped jacket hung on the back of her chair.

Scarlett burst out laughing at the description. Going to court necessitated a certain staid look, and Leigh not only knew it, she followed the unspoken rules on the days she had to do the same. Even today, Leigh wore a pair of dark trousers, a white camisole, and a blazer. No doubt she had her own short dress to change into later.

Having accepted her fate, Scarlett smiled. "You now have control over our plans tonight and my clothing. Are you happy?"

Letting out a clap and squeal, Leigh nodded. "Did I mention I have a bag full of makeup too?"

Scarlett chuckled, giving in to the inevitable. Leigh was right. She only turned thirty once, and Scarlett hadn't gone out for fun in way too long. She missed acting her age and putting her focus on herself and not the job. One night at a club wouldn't kill her. In fact, she might just enjoy it.

"I'm going to close up my computer for the night. I'll meet you in the ladies' room in five minutes." Leigh tapped on her Apple watch. "Don't make me have to come drag you away from paperwork, birthday girl."

"I'll be there," she said to Leigh's retreating back.

Knowing she was now going out tonight, she picked up her cell and called her mother, wanting to check in with her caregiver. For as long as Scarlett could remember, Maxine Davis had suffered from depression. Her father had worked hard at his job as a salesman. Before being relegated to a desk job, he used to travel often and hadn't had a lot of understanding of his wife's moods and inability to function.

He'd taken her to a few doctors, medication had been prescribed, but the drugs didn't work and her mother often forgot to take them. And with her dad busy, her treatment wasn't the best. By the time Scarlett was old enough to comprehend her mother's issues, the depression was deep-seated and no medications took hold or worked. The doctors talked about giving her shock therapy but her mother refused, and as she wasn't a danger to herself or others, no one could force her to agree. Mack, Scarlett's father, took the night shift caring for his wife, and during the day, he paid a neighbor who had been a nurse to watch over her mom.

The phone rang twice and Colleen, the nurse, answered. "Hello?"

"Hi, it's Scarlett. I'm just calling to check on my mom. Is she okay?"

"Hi, honey. Your mom is fine."

Code for status quo. Staring out the window, probably. Scarlett sighed. "Ask her if she wants to talk to me?"

Why she put herself through this, she didn't know. The answer was always the same. Scarlett heard Colleen ask and silence followed.

"I think she's tired," Colleen said gently.

"Thanks." Scarlett swallowed over the lump in her throat. "Tell Dad if he needs me to call."

"I will. You take care," Colleen said.

"You too." Scarlett disconnected and glanced again

at the picture of her brother. She couldn't bring him back any more than she could her mother. Both were lost to her and had been for some time. At least with Hank, she felt like she was accomplishing something in his honor. Putting criminals away, unlike the bastards who'd killed him and gotten away with it.

✧ ✧ ✧

TANNER GRAYSON STEPPED out of the MMA cage, sweating and breathing hard after working out with his sparring opponent. His blood pumped inside him, and his heart beat out a rapid rhythm as he pulled out his mouth guard and tried to catch his breath. Removing his helmet, he shook his head and sweat sprayed around him.

Beside him, his partners and best friends, Jason Dare and Landon Bennett, men he considered brothers, scowled as they did before and after every match or practice Tanner participated in. But they understood, as Tanner did, that working out his aggression was therapy for his anger issues. Hell, it was therapist *approved*.

Kicking, punching, grappling, anything that ultimately involved full-body contact in a channeled way was a relief to his senses. Better than nearly killing a human being in anger, and his partners understood that. They still liked to show up and have his back. Just as he'd always have theirs. He owed them his life. Jason had called in a favor when Tanner had hit rock bottom. His friends had saved him and he'd never forget it. He'd never fuck up what they'd created together.

"Good job," Jason said, handing Tanner his water bottle.

Tanner squeezed it over his face and head before drinking what was left.

Landon passed him a towel and slapped him on the back. "Feel okay?"

Tanner nodded. "Thanks for being here. Let me take a quick shower and we can go grab something to eat before we head over to the club for the night." Tanner jogged into the locker room area, leaving his friends behind.

A short while later, he rejoined them and immediately noticed the change in atmosphere, the tight set to Jason's shoulders, and Landon's steely-eyed stare. Something had clearly occurred while he was cleaning up.

Tanner's entire body tensed as he went on alert. "What happened?"

"Another incident at the club," Landon bit out.

"Fuck," Tanner muttered. They'd had a string of not-so-random problems that had been escalating.

Ever since they'd expanded the club with live acts

and had become an even bigger presence in the Manhattan night scene, someone had been screwing with them. From issues with the sound system that they'd at first attributed to hackers, to automobile vandalism in their parking lot, which had caused them to upgrade the security system and add outdoor cameras, it had become clear that someone wanted to hurt their business.

After the smashing of windows in the parking lot, they'd accompanied their guard outside and found one of the kids with a bat in hand. In exchange for not reporting him to the cops, they'd discovered he and his pals had been paid well by Daniel Sutherland, an owner of a nearby club that wasn't nearly as successful as Club TEN29, to cause trouble.

Tanner had wanted to have a talk with Daniel Sutherland, the owner, but the guys had outvoted him. No one wanted to risk him losing his temper, and Tanner had to agree they were right to hold him back. Instead they'd sent their security to issue a warning. None of them wanted to involve the police unless they had to. Tanner's blood ran hot at the thought that, once again, someone was sabotaging their hard work.

As if sensing he needed calm, Jason put a hand on Tanner's shoulder. "Let's get over there and see what's going on. Then we can work out a plan."

With a nod, Tanner followed his friends out. They

called for an Uber, waited, and climbed into the large SUV, driving to the club in silence, each lost in their own thoughts.

For Tanner, Club TEN29 and his friends were his lifeline. Best friends since meeting in college and experiencing tragedy together and now full partners, they ran the club like a well-oiled machine. Tanner dealt with everything inside the club, Landon handled entertainment, and Jason held the position of CEO, dealing with the business end of things. Although they each had carved out positions, they also jumped in and lent a hand when needed. Decisions were made by the three of them together and it worked. For a club that was a mere two and a half years old, they'd created something to be proud of.

Something Landon's twin, Levi, who'd died in a hazing incident their freshman year in college, would have loved. The club was named after Levi, TEN29 being the month and day he'd died. Everything they did was to make their friend and *brother* proud.

Tanner's anger issues stemmed from his father's verbal abuse and Tanner's inability to fight back against the authority figure his father had been. And certainly his problems with anger had escalated after the night Levi died, but it wasn't something Tanner liked to dwell on now. He just wasn't going to let someone undermine all their hard work.

They pulled up to the club and met their security guard, who had just come on duty, outside.

"Hey, Glenn. What's the problem?" Jason asked.

"Come around back." The big, bald man gestured around the corner, and they followed him to the brick wall on the side of the building where Jason and Landon had parked their vehicles. Both the wall and cars had been spray-painted with graffiti.

Tanner swore at the bright colors on his Range Rover. "What the hell? Sutherland thinks he's going to shut us down with this kind of bullshit?" He shook his head. "It's a pain in the ass but it's manageable. What's his endgame with this kind of annoying harassment?"

"Beats me," Landon muttered. "But look at my fucking car!" He gestured to the Mercedes covered with spray paint.

Hands in his pants pocket, Jason stared at his Jag and shook his head. "Son of a bitch."

Tanner glanced at his friends. "You guys are off tonight, so call to have your cars towed and get out of here. I'll ask our security company to pull the video footage and see what they find, and I'll get Sam Fremont in to cover over the wall before anyone sees. You guys go do your thing."

It was Tanner's night to cover the club, or at least stick around the upstairs apartment. Jason had his wife, Faith, to go home to, and Landon deserved his night off too.

After taking care of their vehicles, the guys left, and Tanner headed upstairs to the apartment they kept above the club. He left a message for Tyler Germaine, the owner of Germaine Security, to check the outside video camera footage in the morning, then changed into the clothes he wore to walk the club floor during business hours.

Dressed and ready, he headed back downstairs for a long night of music, dancing, and hopefully plenty of repeat and new customers having fun and enjoying Club TEN29.

SCARLETT PUT THE glass to her lips and tossed back the frozen vodka shot, her third of the night. "You can multiply that by ten and call it a day," she informed Leigh with a laugh. "Thirty, get it? But no more birthday shots for me." From now on, she'd be nursing a drink and dancing.

She rose to her feet, taking a second to steady herself in her heels, and pulled at the little black skirt Leigh had lent her because it tended to inch up around her thighs. She was feeling ditzy but not totally drunk, and she had to admit coming here tonight had been a good idea.

The club atmosphere was fun. The live singer was

an up-and-coming pop star, or so she'd been told by the friendly bartender. And Leigh was flirting up a storm with a guy she'd met once before and had been texting with ever since. Scarlett didn't think it was coincidence he was here tonight. She'd obviously planned to meet up with him.

"Can I get you something else?" the bartender, a sexy man with his hair buzzed on the sides and longer on top, asked, leaning over the bar to get closer to her.

Although she could admire his looks, he wasn't her type. Too long, lean, and blond. She sighed because it just didn't matter. She had no time for any man in her life right now. "I'll have a pink lemonade on ice, please."

"Gotcha." He snatched up a tip from another customer and turned to work on her order, handing her a glass a few seconds later.

"It's so warm in here," Leigh said, waving her hand in front of her face.

"I think it's all the alcohol you consumed. You're flushed. Do you want to go outside for a few minutes?" Scarlett asked her friend.

She shook her head. "I don't want to leave Cliff alone for some other woman to swoop in and grab him." She tipped her head toward the tall, dark-haired man who was ordering himself a drink and Leigh a glass of water.

Good. Her friend needed a break from drinking.

Looking around, Scarlett studied the mirrored and dark wood bar, turning to check out the other sights just as an elevator door across the way opened. A well-built man dressed in a black suit, with thick jet-black hair and a scruff of beard covering a definitely handsome face stepped out. His imposing and commanding presence couldn't be denied. Now *he* was her type.

"Who is that?" she asked Leigh.

Her friend followed her gaze. "Ooh, that's one of the owners. They're all freaking hot." She waved a hand in front of her face again, this time for a different reason.

Cliff handed her the water glass and said, "Wait for me here? I'll be right back." After pausing to kiss her cheek, he strode away.

Scarlett raised an eyebrow. "Now that's interesting."

"Forget me. *He's* staring at *you*."

"Who?"

"The sexy owner, that's who."

Stunned into silence, Scarlett shifted her stare, and sure enough, hot guy had his eyes laser focused on her. Now that he'd moved closer and she got a better look, she realized words like hot or sexy just didn't cover this man's rougher, rugged looks. Not a pretty boy like the bartender but an Alpha male through and through.

His shoulders were wide and broad, his expression dark as his eyes drank her in. His interest was stamped all over his face, interrupted only when an employee with a drink tray stopped to talk to him.

"Now that's some serious lust at first sight," Leigh said into her ear, talking over the din of the crowd.

Scarlett somehow managed a laugh, because her body was in heated overload due to that chemistry. "Yeah. Too bad I have no time in my life–"

"For a good fuck?" Leigh rolled her eyes. "Come on, Scarlett. Nobody's asking you to date and marry the man. But when was the last time you indulged?" She didn't have to explain what she meant.

"Brian," Scarlett admitted. Her on-again, off-again boyfriend who'd become permanently off when her work schedule increased and was too much for him to handle.

"Well, that's a pathetically long time. And *he's* staring again."

Scarlett met his gaze and her brain buzzed with hormones she'd packed away eight months ago. And she knew the thrill racing around inside her had nothing to do with the alcohol she'd consumed and everything to do with the sizzling promise in the stranger's eyes.

"It's your birthday," her friend reminded her. "Why not treat yourself? Hmm?"

Scarlett drew a deep breath, the rational, smart part of her brain telling her she was an upstanding assistant district attorney with a huge caseload and a mountain of work. She couldn't let herself be distracted. But the female part of her mind and body reminded her of exactly how long it had been since she'd *indulged*. And every instinct she possessed told her she'd never had the kind of dirty sex she'd wind up experiencing with this man.

As her inner good girl warred with the bad girl inside her, Leigh whispered, "Happy birthday," in her ear.

"That's it. I'm going for it," Scarlett decided. Didn't she deserve a night off? A selfish grab of time before she dove back into her crazy life?

"Yes!" Leigh's fist pump made Scarlett laugh.

The problem was she couldn't remember the last time she'd come onto a man with the express intent of taking him home. Or vice versa.

Turning to the bartender, she said, "Can I get another shot please?"

"Sure thing, pretty lady." He poured the vodka and slid the small glass toward her.

After drawing a deep breath, she downed the liquor for courage. "Happy birthday to me," she muttered under her breath.

"You know our drill. You text me tonight no matter what."

Scarlett nodded. She and Leigh had been working together for three years, four if you counted the fact that they'd both interned at the district attorney's office the summer before graduation from law school. They'd had plenty of nights out and safety checks in place.

"On it," Scarlett promised.

Then she turned back to the man who mattered to find him in deep conversation with someone who looked like one of the bodyguards around the establishment. But she quickly realized he still was aware of where *she* was when he met her gaze once more, this time a sinful smile lifting the corners of his mouth.

Taking the gesture as an invitation, she whispered to Leigh, "Wish me luck," and started across the club floor.

Although he still spoke to the other man, his eyes were blatantly on hers, causing her to add a seductive swing to her hips and a toss of her hair over her shoulders as she approached.

The moment she stepped up to him, he cut off his conversation and his eyes locked with hers. Desire, swift and furious, flowed through her veins, reassuring her she was making the right choice with this guy.

"I'm Scarlett," she said, foregoing last names for the kind of night she had in mind.

Chapter Two

"TANNER." HIS VOICE came out gravelly and raw as he exchanged names with the gorgeous female he'd noticed the second he'd stepped out of the elevator. He couldn't recall the last time just the sight of a woman had impacted him so strongly.

At a glance, even with her wearing a tight short skirt, she stood out in the crowd as a woman with class. Her sandy-blonde hair was full, thick, and fell below her shoulders in a sweeping caress. Those hot pink lips made her mouth ripe for kissing. Add the sleek black liner around her eyes, and she was a knockout. A woman who oozed sophistication beneath the clothing and one who belonged in a five-star restaurant and not a nightclub, no matter how much Tanner appreciated the atmosphere they'd built here.

She was definitely out of his league, not that he gave a shit. If he'd learned one thing in his life, it was to live in and appreciate the moment because tomorrow wasn't guaranteed.

"Can I buy you a drink?" he asked, the fire crackling between them so alive he was surprised everyone around them couldn't feel the heat.

She slicked her tongue over her bottom lip and his cock pulsed at the not-so-innocent gesture. "I was hoping you'd take me to bed."

He narrowed his gaze, taken aback by her brazen words. "Don't get me wrong, gorgeous. I'd like nothing more, but you don't strike me as the type of woman to pick up strange men in a bar." She was more a wine-and-dine kind of female.

A flush rose to her cheeks. "Okay, maybe you've pegged me right but it's my birthday. Can't a girl step outside the box when she decides to celebrate?"

Reaching out, she lifted his tie in one hand and pulled him closer, giving him a look into green eyes with flecks of gold. So close her peach scent assaulted his senses, ramping up his desire.

"Correct me if I'm wrong but there's some serious chemistry between us," she murmured.

"Damn right there is." He felt the pull between them as strongly as the hold she had on his tie.

"So are you going to act on it?" She obviously meant the words as a challenge.

And he was hesitating? What the fuck was wrong with him? True, he'd grown bored of the women throwing themselves at him because he owned Club TEN29. Sex was easy for him if and when he desired it. But here was an incredible woman offering herself to him on a silver platter. She stood out from all the others and he wanted her beneath him badly.

Maybe Jason or Landon would do the noble thing, but he'd always been the bad boy of the bunch, and though he'd left behind his issues, the remnants of that man remained.

Enough to take her up on her proposition. "This way. I have an apartment upstairs." He placed a hand on her lower back, guiding her, but an instant later, his conscience tugged at him, and he ducked into a shadow of a hallway, pulling her body flush against his.

She was soft and pillowy, all sweet-smelling woman, and his dick throbbed in his pants as he backed her against the wall, their bodies flush against each other.

"Why are you stopping here?" she asked.

He placed his hand beneath her chin and tipped her head up to meet his gaze. "Just making sure you're sober and know what you want."

A flicker of surprise flashed in her gaze. "So you've got a little bit of a gentleman behind the gruff exterior." She slid her hand through his hair, pulling on the longish strands. "I'm a big girl, Tanner. I know what I want. And I want you."

✧   ✧   ✧

SCARLETT DIDN'T KNOW where her sudden burst of

courage came from, but she wasn't about to turn away now. Not when she had the sexiest man she'd ever laid eyes on ready to take her to bed. Her body trembled with desire and an awareness that something special was about to happen between them. Especially with the way Tanner's eyes darkened at her bold, certain words of reassurance.

Grasping her hand, he led her back into the main room and to the elevator he'd walked out of earlier. He hit a button and the doors slid open. No sooner were they enclosed in the small area than she found herself surrounded by the sensual scent of his masculine cologne and by the man himself.

He hit the floor number, then backed her against the wall and braced his hips against hers. The hardness of his erection pressed into her sex, and she moaned at the anticipation of what was to come, her underwear growing damp with arousal.

"Make no mistake. You might have been the one to convince me but I'm taking control now."

No man in her past ever spoke to her in such a self-assured, dominant way. To her surprise, she liked it. Hell, her perky nipples were proof of that, and he was looking down at the evidence with dilated pupils. Before she could respond, the elevator dinged and the doors slid open.

Holding her hand once more, he led her down a

short hall and unlocked the sole door. She stepped into the apartment, which was smaller than she'd anticipated, realizing immediately he didn't live here. There were no personal effects anywhere on the shelves, and the steel and white décor gave a sterile feeling to the place.

The door shut behind them.

"We share the apartment, my partners and I," he said, as if reading her mind. "Whoever has the night shift uses it if they don't feel like going home late. Although since Jason got married, it's just me and Landon."

She looked around once more. "It's beautiful. Just very empty," she murmured.

He shrugged, sliding his jacket off his broad shoulders. "It serves a purpose."

"Do you bring many women up here?" she asked, unable to withhold her curiosity. After all, he was a hot guy with easy access to a bed above where he worked.

His sharp gaze slid to hers. "None. At least not anymore." He hesitated before going on. "I admit when we first opened the club, the women throwing themselves at me were a novelty that I indulged, but after a while, they all seemed to have an agenda."

"Such as?" she asked.

"They assumed because I owned the club I had money, and they wanted to be the woman on my arm permanently."

His voice turned bitter and she didn't blame him. "You don't have to worry about that with me. My job and my life are too full to want anything more than one night."

A sinful smile curved his lips. "So I'm your birthday present?"

She nodded. "And I can't wait to unwrap you." Making good on her words, she reached up and began to unbutton his shirt, working her way down, taking one at a time, exposing his olive skin and a smattering of dark chest hair.

Her pulse thudded harder as she reached the waistband of his pants. After pulling up the ends of the shirt, she released the last button and slid the material over his shoulders. He dropped the garment onto the floor. Faced with the muscles she'd only imagined, she looked her fill, in awe of the definition that showed that he had to work out in order to have that kind of physique.

"You like what you see."

It wasn't a question and she didn't play coy. "I do." Drawing on the rest of her courage, she placed a hand over the bulge in his pants. His cock pulsed against her hand, and need swept over her in a raging fire she couldn't control.

Yet she managed to play out the fantasy of unwrapping her gift. "Now let's see the rest of you." She worked the fastening of his slacks, undid the zipper, taking care because she realized she wasn't dealing with a small man.

The material slid to the floor, leaving him in boxer briefs that showed the outline of a very impressive package.

"You realize I'm letting you lead because I'm your present," he said through gritted teeth. "But if you go much slower, I'm going to explode before we get to the good stuff."

She laughed but she understood he was serious. "I'm almost there," she promised, hooking her fingers into the sides of his briefs, pulling them down, and exposing his huge, thick cock to her waiting gaze. "Best birthday present ever," she said as she eased the boxer briefs down his legs.

They dropped to the floor and he kicked them off, then bent and swept her into his arms. "My turn. Except I'm not only going to undress you, I'm going to taste every delectable inch of your skin."

Holy hell, she'd underestimated this man, she thought as she wrapped her arms around him for the quick walk to the bedroom. Unable to stop herself, she put her face in the crook of his neck and drew in a deep breath, inhaling his scent and memorizing it for the future. When she was alone and had this night to remember.

He deposited her on the bed, her shoes falling before she even landed, and he immediately began to undress her. No slow unwrapping for her. He pulled her skirt off, the elastic waist making it easy for him to ease it over her legs and onto the floor. Shocking her, he'd hooked his fingers into the waistband of her panties and now she was bared to him, only her camisole covering her.

He stood at the edge of the bed, situated between her legs, and picked up one foot and kissed her ankle. She blinked. And he licked and kissed his way up the rest of her leg and calf, making good on his promise of tasting every inch of her. Whether she was delectable or not, she didn't know, but his eyes blazed with hunger as he worked his way to his ultimate destination.

Grasping her thighs in each hand, he ran his tongue along the seam of her thigh and her sex, causing her to tremble with yearning, a pulsing desire sweeping through her. That tongue continued its leisurely path traveling up and over her belly, then working its way to the other side and repeating his teasing ministrations.

Dying. She was dying for him to lick her sex. Her clit. To tongue her and make her come. This wasn't the kind of sex she was used to. Quick, dark room, *we're in a relationship and overdue*, that was her past. She could quickly get used to this kind of thorough man. One who made her burn.

She arched her hips and silently urged him to move where she wanted him to go.

"Looking for relief?" he asked, his voice a husky chuckle.

"You could say that."

"You didn't think I'd make you pay for the way you slowly stripped off my clothes?" He raised an eyebrow, letting her know he was in control of this scenario.

Again, despite the throbbing in her core, she liked knowing he'd give her what he wanted when he was good and ready. She had a hunch it would only make the end that much sweeter.

"You said you were in charge." Her voice shook as she spoke.

"I am. And I just realized I haven't kissed you yet."

She slid her tongue over her lips, wishing it was his tongue, his mouth. "Nope. Going to kiss you here first." He dipped his head and swiped his tongue over her clit.

She threw her head back against the mattress and moaned. After that, she lost track of everything but his talented mouth as he did so much more than kiss her. He devoured her, licking her up one side of her sex and down the other, teasing with his teeth, soothing with his tongue, teasing her clit, and bringing her to the brink before easing off and going back to tormenting her in other ways with his lips and tongue.

Soon she was writhing beneath him, grinding herself against his mouth, begging for relief that was just out of reach. His beard scratched her thighs, her sex, her clit, and she was so close to climax she could taste it.

Without warning, he slid a finger inside her and she jolted beneath him. She hadn't known how much she needed to be filled until she felt him stretch inside her. She whimpered and he pulled out, thrusting back in with what felt like two fingers, curling them against her inner walls.

"Tanner!" she screamed as she came, the sound of his name on her lips feeling so natural and right. Ripples and waves of delicious sensation washed over her, and as he pumped his fingers in and out, her climax continued until she collapsed against the mattress in a sated heap.

She wasn't sure how much time passed before her breathing returned to normal and she opened her eyes to find a dark-eyed Tanner staring at her, a satisfied smile on his face.

"What are you grinning at?" she asked, squeezing her legs together, which only served to spike her arousal, a shocking discovery, given how hard she'd just come.

"Just thinking about how much I enjoyed that."

She blinked. "Really? Because it's not like you—"

"Oh, we'll get to that. I've decided it's my goal to make this your best birthday ever."

"Since the actual day is tomorrow, you have plenty of time to do just that."

He tossed his head back and laughed. "I like you, Scarlett."

She grinned. "From what I know of you, I like you too, Tanner."

A hooded look shuttered his eyes, and a muscle ticked in his jaw, making her wonder what she'd said to kill his good mood. Before she could ask, he was grinning again, less real this time, but she allowed him his private thoughts. After all, this wasn't more than a one-night stand. She didn't have the right to dig into his feelings. Despite the fact that she had the ridiculous desire to know more about him.

Reminding herself of the commitments that awaited her in her real life, both personal and professional, that left her no time for anything more, she forced her attention back to what tonight was about. Sex. Raw, hungry sex.

Deciding they both needed to focus on now, she reached out and grasped his shaft in her hand, feeling the silken thickness for the first time. As she wrapped her hand around him and slid her palm up and down, her fingers didn't meet and she realized she was in for a hard ride. Jesus. Would he even fit? she wondered, her hand stilling.

"Something wrong?"

She bit the inside of her cheek. "It's been awhile and you're big." Her cheeks flushed at the admission.

"I promise I won't hurt you." He pushed himself up and over her, the flex of his biceps something to see, and laid his big body on top of her. "Now let me have a real kiss," he said, sealing their lips together.

His kiss was hot and needy, his tongue as silken in her mouth as it had been on her sex, his technique as talented. He knew how to make her forget everything but the touch and feel of him as he rocked his body against hers. His mouth mimicked the sexual act, his body bucking and arching beneath her while his cock pulsed against her lower abdomen.

Need coursed through her veins and kissing him wasn't enough. As if he read her mind, he rolled over and reached for the nightstand, opening the drawer and pulling out a condom. Before she could react, he'd ripped open the foil and rolled the protection over himself. While he did his thing, she removed her cami and unhooked her bra, tossing them to the floor, where her skirt and panties lay.

Then he was back, his blue-gray gaze wide as he took in her breasts. "You're a feast for the eyes," he said, leaning down and licking first one of her nipples, then the other.

She moaned and he settled on top of her, his body poised at her entrance. Those thick arms were braced on either side of her, his eyes serious on hers. "You with me?" he asked.

She nodded, arching her hips to let him know she wanted him inside her. He pushed in slowly but she was wet and ready for him, and despite his thickness and girth, her body accepted him, if not easily, then readily, as he pushed in and retreated, in farther, only to pull out again.

With every thrust, she took more of him, his gaze darkening with each deeper dive inside her until finally he was all the way home. Her eyelids fluttered open and she met his intense stare. His thick cock pulsed inside her, filling her so completely she was seconds from coming again.

If he moved, she'd come apart. Never before had she experienced such an all-encompassing sensation. This man was different than anyone she'd been with. He was setting the bar so high she'd never experience anything like him again. Which meant she was going to enjoy every second.

"We're good?" He kissed her nose and she melted

beneath him.

"We're good. Now move."

He chuckled at her demand. But he listened. From the gentleman worried about hurting her, he turned into the dominant man he'd promised he'd be. He pulled out and slammed into her again. And again, picking up a rhythm that immediately had her inner walls clasping around him, tremors taking hold as he hit the sensitive spot inside her he'd already found with his fingers. She started to come, her entire body arching and spasming around him.

Bright lights sparkled behind her eyes and her orgasm hit her hard. It didn't end fast, either. As he pounded his big body inside her, he kept the tremors coming, overtaking her body, her mind, her soul. And while she came, she called his name over and over again.

✧   ✧   ✧

TANNER WOKE WITH a start, the vibrating buzzer on his phone startling him. He came to, a soft, sweet woman wrapped around him, and he realized he didn't want to answer the call. That was a first, since nothing came before the club. His business. His partners.

Priorities that had been beaten into him the night he hadn't listened to his gut and let Levi lead them into a nightmare. Now? His partners or club needed him? He jumped into action.

He disentangled himself from Scarlett and climbed out of bed naked, pulling his phone from his pants pocket. A glance at the text told him there'd been a dispute downstairs. They needed him.

"What's wrong?" She sat up in bed, pulling the covers with her, covering the sexy body he'd learned intimately. More than once.

After the first time, they'd been insatiable, discovering each other in different ways, many times over. All of it hadn't been like him. Normally sex satisfied him and he was done.

A glance at the female with the tousled blonde hair and the wide green eyes staring uncertainly at him and he knew he was far from finished with her. She might be out of his league, something he'd pegged at a glance, but that didn't mean he wouldn't hold on while he enjoyed what they shared.

"There's a problem downstairs," he said, reaching for his boxers and pulling them on. They'd only slept for about an hour. His pants came next. "I'll go deal with the situation. Make yourself at home. There's food in the fridge or you can rest here. I'll be back."

"But—"

Before she could argue, he stalked over to her side of the bed, leaned down, and covered her mouth with his, kissing her until hopefully she forgot any objections she had to staying put.

Pulling back, he took in her dazed gaze with satisfaction. "I'm not finished with you, birthday girl."

She blinked up at him. "Okay," she whispered.

He nodded and rose, heading to the closet and pulling out a sweater. He wasn't going to bother putting on a wrinkled shirt and taking the time to button it. He needed to see what the hell was going on in the club.

But not before he stole one more kiss from the woman in his bed.

THE APARTMENT DOOR slammed shut and Scarlett dove for her phone. Just as she realized on wakening, there were a bunch of texts from Leigh, worried because Scarlett hadn't checked in. The last one noted that because she knew Scarlett had gone upstairs with Tanner, Leigh assumed she was safe but she was going to kill her when she heard from Scarlett in the morning.

Wincing, she texted Leigh that she was fine but she'd fallen asleep before she could check in. Leigh immediately replied and Scarlett's guilt dissipated a little.

Now she glanced around, realizing she was naked in a stranger's apartment. Not really a stranger, considering how well he'd learned her body but a stranger nevertheless. He wanted her to wait for him.

She wanted to be here when he returned. But the truth was, they'd agreed on one night and she *liked* him. Forget the hot body and gorgeous face, he had a solid strength to him she admired, a generosity in his sexual activities that was rare, and a dominant aspect to him that appealed to her. She wanted to get to know him better, and she had no time in her life for a man or a relationship.

The memory of the caseload of work waiting for her returned, along with the mother she felt responsible for and who she visited on her rare time off. How could she stay and let herself get involved with a man she knew she could develop feelings for?

With a shake of her head and a sad sigh, she reached for her clothes and quickly dressed, not wanting to run into Tanner coming back. That would make for an awkward conversation she didn't want to have.

She picked up her phone and called for an Uber. And though she debated leaving him a note, that would lead to further contact and that wouldn't be fair to either of them. One night. No time. She had to go.

Now she just had to hope she could slip out of the club without running into Tanner. She took the elevator down and stepped out into the still busy club.

She didn't know how he kept these hours but he must be used to them. Looking around, she saw him talking to a security guard and a group of unhappy customers in the far corner of the club.

Feeling guilty but determined, she rushed through the club and headed out the front door and into the dark night. Her Uber was waiting, the driver repeating her name to her before she climbed into the back of the car, shutting the door and putting Tanner behind her.

Except during the ride home, she couldn't forget the night she'd had, the sexy, forceful way he'd taken her, and how much she'd enjoyed every second she'd spent with him. She owed Leigh for convincing her to go out or she'd never have had such an incredible night.

Happy birthday to me, she thought, as the car took her farther away from the club and the man she'd never forget.

Chapter Three

TANNER HATED DEALING with escalating disputes, but that was part of his job. He especially hated leaving the warm, willing woman upstairs in his bed to remind assholes that his club was an upscale establishment and he wouldn't tolerate bullshit. If his security couldn't get the people involved to willingly leave, Tanner or one of the other partners came down and banned them from the club for good. Luckily they didn't need to call the cops in on this one, and eventually the douchebags left the premises.

But he'd been gone over forty minutes by the time he headed back upstairs, and he discovered his apartment and his bed empty. He ran a hand through his hair as he studied the rumpled sheets, the memory of the gorgeous blonde making his dick rise.

Shit.

He'd really wanted to go another round or two. And that wasn't his typical MO. He ought to be happy she was gone, making the morning after easier on them both. Instead his stomach was churning with disappointment. What the hell was that about?

He pulled off his sweater and stripped naked, sliding between the now cool sheets that still smelled of sex and Scarlett. He had to admit, her disappearing on him had taken him off guard. It stung his ego, yes, because for sure he'd been interested in her as maybe even more than a one-night stand. But obviously she'd been thinking differently. Hell, she'd said as much when he'd admitted to getting bored of the club bunnies who wanted something from him afterwards. So maybe he got what he deserved with her pulling a vanishing act.

He placed his hand behind his head and stared at the ceiling, unable to fall asleep. Eventually he must have dozed off because the light streaming through the window woke him in the morning.

He stretched, covered his morning wood with his hand, pissed again that Scarlett had bailed on him. She'd been sassy with how she'd approached him, refreshingly honest in what she wanted, clearly smart, and fun. And he didn't even know her last name.

He shook his head, further annoyed with himself for how he'd let the night play out. He should have asked more questions in case he wanted to see her again. Of course, he did own the club, and if she'd paid by credit card, he could pull last night's receipts and search for her unique first name. That would give him her last name.

Not that a last name in a place as big as Manhattan would enable him to find her. Assuming she even lived in the city.

Fuck.

Glancing to the side of the bed where she'd been, his gaze fell on a simple gold chain lying by the pillows. Picking it up, he turned it over in his hand, noticing a small heart that links had broken off of. It wasn't an expensive item and it was interesting to him that Scarlett wore something so delicate and fragile.

But as he examined the piece, he realized that *now* she'd have a reason to return to the club, assuming the bracelet meant something to her. Tanner wasn't a big believer in hope, but it was all he had at the moment. Hope that Scarlett would come back to find her missing jewelry.

✧   ✧   ✧

SCARLETT CAME HOME and showered, then climbed into bed and fell into a deep sleep. She woke up, sore in the best possible ways, thanks to Tanner. She might not make it a habit of sleeping with men she just met but she couldn't regret her night with him.

Wearing nothing but her robe and a cropped tee shirt underneath, she headed for the kitchen and poured herself a glass of orange juice and drank while she popped a K-cup into the coffee brewer. A few minutes later, she sat with her coffee and a protein bar, staring at her laptop screen.

She needed to check email because her boss didn't stop working just because it was the weekend, but she was tempted to look up Club TEN29 and see what she could learn about one owner in particular. Her fingers hesitated over the keyboard and she stopped herself, opening her mail program instead. She and Tanner had agreed on one night, and besides, if she learned more about him, she'd only be more curious and want to get to know him better. No time. Not happening.

A peek at her email showed her nothing had come in overnight, so her best bet was to begin to prep the next case. She finished her mug of coffee, rinsed out the cup, and placed it on the counter when her phone dinged. She knew it had to be Leigh, and after a happy birthday exchange, she settled in for a long discussion on last night's events but found she wanted to keep the details to herself.

What she had shared with Tanner was a night out of time, something special she'd always cherish. She wanted to hold it close to her heart and keep it safe. She didn't want to talk about it, even with her best friend, so she left things as vague as possible in her texts, but she couldn't hide the fact that the night had meant something to her.

She placed her phone on the table and glanced at her wrist, realizing for the first time her bracelet was gone. Her stomach twisted and her eyes filled with tears. "Hank."

She drew a deep breath and rushed around her apartment, checking her bedroom, bed, the floors, the bathroom, and the shower. Assuming it hadn't gone down the drain, it wasn't here.

Sitting down on the bed, she forced herself to calm down and think. "When was the last time I saw it on my wrist?"

She recalled looking at it in the office late yesterday. And she'd noticed it when she paid the bill last night, reaching her hand across the counter to give the bartender her credit card. Which meant the bracelet was either in the club or in Tanner's bed.

She closed her eyes and groaned. With no choice, she Googled Club TEN29 on her phone and dialed the club's number, avoiding the About page that would tell her anything about Tanner, the man she couldn't get out of her head.

✧　✧　✧

AROUND NOON, TANNER pounded downstairs in a pissed-off mood. On top of Scarlett's disappearance, the security company hadn't checked the footage from last night yet, setting Tanner off even more.

He bit the head off of the cleaning crew that got in his way, then pulled the credit card receipts just because he could. The stack would take him hours to go through, and Scarlett could just as easily have paid in cash. Then he'd have to find a needle in a haystack, searching for her in every borough.

"Stalker much?" he muttered to himself, wondering how this one woman had gotten to him so badly that the thought of never seeing her again was like a punch in the gut.

"Hey." Jason joined him at the bar, sliding into the stool beside him. "I heard the staff talking. What bit you in the ass this morning?"

"Yeah, well, they were under my feet and annoying the shit out of me."

Jason narrowed his gaze. "Why didn't you just go upstairs and hang in the offices until they were gone?"

"Because I had something to do. What's with the third degree?" Tanner braced an elbow on the bar and faced his friend.

"What's with the credit card receipts all over the counter?" Jason asked.

Tanner groaned and swiped a hand over his face. Screw it. If he was going to admit what was bothering him to anyone, it might as well be the friend who was already in deep with a woman, not the one who wouldn't understand.

"I met a woman." He didn't need to say more.

Jason would understand how profound a statement that was. "Yeah? What's her name?"

"Scarlett."

"Pretty name. Scarlett what's her last name? Who introduced you? Why are you in such a piss-poor mood then?" His friend shot off the questions as they came to him.

"I stepped off the elevator last night and I lost my fucking breath. That was it. Stupid cliché but we locked eyes and I was done for."

Jason shook his head and laughed.

"What's so funny?" Tanner had thought, of all people, Jason would understand.

Jason placed a brotherly hand on Tanner's shoulder. "I was laughing because it was Faith's ass I saw first but forget about me. That's seriously how it happens. One minute you're going about your life and the next you're knocked off your feet. So again, what's the problem?" He leaned back in his chair and waited for an answer.

"We didn't exchange last names, we went upstairs, I got a call from the club, and when I came back to the apartment, she was gone."

"Hence the credit card receipts." Jason's gaze scanned the counter. "Any luck?"

"I'm wasting my time. A last name's not going to

get me anywhere in a city this size. I'm just doing it to feel like I'm doing *something*."

"Hey, boss! Phone call," Felicia, their daytime hostess, called. They liked to keep someone at the club to handle calls and schedule parties.

"Which one of us?" Tanner asked.

"You!" Felicia replied.

Tanner headed around the bar and picked up the phone. "Grayson," he barked into the receiver.

"Tanner?" a familiar voice asked and his entire mood brightened.

"Scarlett?" As he spoke, Tanner caught Jason's shit-eating grin from across the counter and gave him the finger.

Jason merely chuckled.

"Hi," she said. "I lost something either at the bar or your apartment, and I was hoping you could keep an eye out?"

"A bracelet?" He'd already put his hand into his front pocket and fingered the delicate chain between his fingertips.

"You found it?" A relieved sigh sounded over the line. "Thank God."

"Sounds like it's important to you," he said, his curiosity definitely piqued.

"You have no idea. If you leave it with someone up front, I can pick it up later today or tomorrow, if that's okay?"

Just the sound of her voice had his heart rate picking up rhythm. "I have a better idea. Give me your address and I'll bring it to you. That way you can explain in private why you ran out on me this morning?"

He heard the huff of breath and the deliberate pause she took before answering. "I thought it would be easier. Smarter."

He narrowed his gaze at both of those honest answers. Easier, he understood. He'd thought as much himself. Smarter? "Let me ask you something." And her answer would determine how he handled her from here.

"Okay," she said warily.

"Did you *want* to stay but thought since we'd agreed on one night it was smarter to leave?" If so, he'd be on his way to her place the second he hung up the phone. "Or did you really want to go before I came back?" In which case he'd leave the bracelet with Felicia and try to forget he'd ever met Scarlett.

She blew out a breath again. "Does it really matter which?"

"Abso-fucking-lutely."

She chuckled at that. "I wanted to stay." There was that honesty again.

"Then give me your address and let me bring you

the bracelet."

"It's really not a good idea. My life is busy and—"

"Address, Scarlett." He wasn't giving in. Her excuses were just that. Clearly she had walls and so what? So did he. That didn't mean he was giving up on her without a fight.

He wanted to get to know this woman better, and since she'd admitted she'd wanted to stay, he felt comfortable pushing past her defenses. Then a thought dawned on him and he decided to offer her an out, his stomach in knots as he asked, "Unless you *really* don't want to see me, in which case I'll leave the bracelet and you'll never hear from me again."

She immediately rattled off her address and apartment number. "I don't have time in my life for you, Tanner—"

"Grayson. Tanner Grayson. And you're Scarlett...?"

"Davis," she muttered, causing him to grin. "Make time, Scarlett Davis. Because I'm coming to get you and give you a birthday celebration you won't soon forget."

"You already did," she said before disconnecting the call.

He couldn't wipe the grin off his face if he wanted to, which had Jason laughing at him from across the bar. He disconnected the call.

"You're so fucked," Jason said. "Welcome to the club."

"I've only known her for a couple of hours," Tanner reminded his friend as well as himself.

"Sometimes that's all it takes."

"Hey, is Sweet Treats open today? And is Faith working?" he asked of Jason's wife's candy shop.

Jason nodded. "Why do you think I'm killing time alone here? Why do you want to know?"

Tanner rolled his eyes but he got it. Jason would rather be spending time with his wife. "Call her and put me on the phone, would you? I have a favor to ask."

After arranging the day, he headed upstairs to make sure he had everything he needed before taking off to meet Scarlett.

✧　✧　✧

SCARLETT RUSHED AROUND her room, picking and discarding outfits like a crazy woman before finally settling on a pair of dark denim skinny jeans and a pink camouflage-designed top with a low vee in the front. Since she had no idea where they were going or how much walking would be involved, she chose a pair of ballet flats for her feet.

Considering the amount of work she had to do for trial, she had to be insane to take an entire day off, and yet when Tanner had promised to leave her alone for good, she'd given him her address so quickly her head still spun. The man had had quite an effect on her.

Enough to allow her to convince herself she deserved her birthday off from work. Then she'd explain to Tanner why she had to focus on her career and let him down gently before she got attached and he dumped her as fast as her ex when she'd had no time for him in her life.

She'd fallen asleep with wet hair last night, so she had big hair today and pulled it up into a messy bun. No sense in scaring the man. And since she didn't wear a lot of makeup, after a few swipes of blush, mascara, and lip gloss, she was ready just as her doorbell rang.

She pressed a hand over the nervous flutters in her stomach and headed to the door, opening it to let Tanner inside. No sooner had he entered and shut the door behind him than he wrapped an arm around her waist, pulled her into him, and pressed his lips to hers.

She melted against him, all the objections and reasons she didn't have time in her life for a man gone the minute his mouth came down on hers. His tongue thrust in and tangled with hers and she was lost in the way he kissed. They stood that way for who knew how long, her hands in his hair, his on her hips, their bodies rocking together until finally he came up for air.

"That was the pent-up frustration from thinking I might never hear from you again. Or find you in this huge city, Scarlett with no last name."

She blew out a slow breath. "Umm, I'm sorry. But I mean it when I say my time is taken up with work. I can't make promises–"

"And I don't want any. I just want to go out today, okay? One day at a time."

She pursed her lips, knowing she'd heard that before. *It's fine, Scarlett. I just want to see you when I can. I'll be around when you're free, Scarlett.* And the truth was? She couldn't even blame Brian for looking elsewhere.

But she wasn't going to give up today with Tanner. She'd agreed to take today off, something she never ever did even on weekends. "Okay. So what's the plan?"

His expression brightened at her question. "That's a surprise. Are you ready?"

"Let me grab my bag." She ran to her room, picked up her pocketbook, slung it over her shoulder, and returned to find him studying pictures on her bookshelf.

"Your family?" he asked, taking in the set on the shelf that was eye-level.

She nodded. "That's my brother. He died when he was sixteen, and that's my mom and dad." She spoke quickly, hoping to bypass any painful conversation.

"I'm sorry," he murmured in her ear. "Your mother doesn't look happy in any of the pictures. Not even the more recent ones."

She swallowed hard. "Mom suffers from severe depression. Major depressive disorder. She doesn't really take part in life." She swallowed past the lump in her throat.

"You've had it hard," he said, pulling her against him.

"Doesn't everyone in one way or another?"

"Good point. So ready to go?" he asked, obviously and abruptly changing subject, which told her he had rough parts of his own past he wasn't looking for her to dig into.

"I am." Turning her back on the pictures and her past, they walked out the door and she locked it behind her.

He called for an Uber as she excitedly bounced on her feet. "So where are we going?" she asked again.

"You don't do surprises well, do you?" he asked with an indulgent grin.

"I don't normally do birthdays." That slipped out, but since she'd already revealed the truth about her mom, she figured she might as well tell him more.

"My mother wasn't capable of remembering things, so I pretty much took care of myself. I mean, Dad worked during the day, and my brother needed me. It wasn't easy for Dad to keep up with things like birthdays or holidays either, so we just didn't. Except Hank. My brother. He remembered my birthday and I remembered his, even if it was a single cupcake with a candle."

She grinned at the memory. "Shortly before he died, it was my birthday and he'd been working at a convenience store in a not-so-great area. But he saved and bought me the bracelet. Oh!" She couldn't believe she'd forgotten the important item in the excitement of seeing Tanner again.

"Here," he said in a gruff voice, putting his hand in his pocket and pulling out the bracelet. "I'm glad I found it for you."

"Thanks." She tucked it safely inside her purse. "I'll get it fixed. I know it's not real but it's all I have left of him."

Before Tanner could ask what happened, the Uber pulled into the circular drive of her apartment building, cutting off conversation. They climbed inside and the car drove to whatever destination Tanner had in mind. And the little girl inside Scarlett, who hadn't had a birthday party that she could recall, was excited and knew that no matter what he had planned, it would be a day she always remembered.

✧　✧　✧

TANNER NOW KNEW more about Scarlett than he'd imagined learning in such a short time. Given what he'd discovered, he was even more determined to give her a fun birthday. No child should be without a birthday celebration. Tanner's dad had been a strict ass and borderline verbally abusive, letting Tanner know in no uncertain terms he'd never amount to anything. But his mom was the best.

And she'd definitely celebrated his and his sister's birthdays. Deciding to give Scarlett a special day seemed only natural to him. Now he was so glad that he had.

First stop? Faith's Sweet Treats.

The car pulled up to a storefront with a variety of shops. They thanked the driver and stepped out.

"Are we going to the candy shop?" she asked.

"We are," he said as he opened the door for her. "Jason's wife, Faith, owns the place."

They stepped inside and delicious smells of sugary treats assaulted them.

"Mmm. Smells so good," she said.

"Agreed."

Faith, a curvy blonde woman wearing a Sweet Treats tee shirt and jeans, came to greet them. "Tanner!" She walked out from behind the counter and pulled him into a hug before turning to Scarlett. "And you must be Scarlett! It's nice to meet you and happy birthday!"

Faith was so sweet it galled Tanner to think of what an asshole he'd been when he'd first met her. He was protective of his friends and he'd been looking out for Jason. Turned out there was no need. Faith was like a ray of sunshine and she was the best thing that had happened to Jason.

Scarlett wrinkled her nose in confusion. "Umm, thank you. How do you know me?" she asked.

Tanner's hand came to rest on her back, the touch intimate and warm. "I called ahead." He winked at Faith, who merely grinned at how they'd conspired.

"Have a seat," Faith said. "I'll be right out with your order."

Seeming a little dazed, Scarlett let him lead her to an open table. They settled into the chairs, side by side.

"What did you do?" she asked him.

"Well, I don't have an in with a bakery but I did here. So instead of a traditional birthday cake, I called in an order for something different." And now he was so fucking glad that he had.

Faith returned, talking as she approached. "So I didn't have much time to go crazy and make anything really unique, but I had the supplies for these," she said, coming up to the table holding a tray of mini sugar cones with ice-cream-designed cake pops in each one.

Scarlett's eyes opened wide at the sight. "They look amazing! Too good to eat!"

"Never," Faith said with a grin. "They're meant for you to enjoy." She placed the tray on the table just as the bell rang over the door again. "Oops, customers." She headed for the counter and Scarlett turned to Tanner.

"You did this for me?"

He nodded, trying not to betray the fact that, in less than a day, this woman had gotten under his skin. He understood better than most that he was damaged goods that most females didn't want once they knew the details about his past.

She blinked back real tears. "Before you really knew me. Before you knew how much something like this would mean to me, you arranged to celebrate."

He reached across the table and took her hand. "You're special. I saw that the second I laid eyes on you. Too damned good for me, that's for sure."

She narrowed her gaze. "From where I'm sitting, you're pretty special yourself, Tanner Grayson."

He let her think it for now.

✧   ✧   ✧

FAITH JOINED THEM when she had a lull in customers, and Scarlett had learned that she'd met Jason when she'd had a flat tire and during a rough time in her life.

At a point when she'd been hiding from her abusive brother, who wanted her inheritance. Jason had stepped up and moved her in with him shortly after they'd met. What had started as insta-lust had become insta-love. The way she spoke about Jason, the sparkle in her eyes, it was almost contagious. Almost. Because although it would be nice to have someone in her life she could count on one hundred percent, to have that, she needed to give it. And she didn't have that kind of time or ability.

"Okay, time to leave," Tanner said, interrupting her thoughts, for which Scarlett was grateful.

"Let me box up the pops," Faith offered. "This way you can take them with you."

A little while later, they were on their way. To Scarlett's surprise, Tanner took her to a place called China Fair, an arcade on Mott Street in Chinatown, where they walked into a shockingly empty place.

"Welcome," an elderly man said, greeting them.

"Hi. I'm Tanner Grayson. Thank you for accommodating me at the last minute."

The man nodded at him. "The place is yours. Minimum of three hours. If you stay longer, I charge you double for closing last minute on a Saturday."

"Understood." Tanner shook the man's hand.

Scarlett opened and closed her mouth, then opted to remain silent. It seemed money could buy anything even at the last minute. She couldn't imagine what it had cost him nor did she want to know. For her, it was the thought that counted.

Tanner gestured into the back room and she walked alongside him, his hand on her lower back, her skin tingling beneath her top. "So what's your game of choice?" he asked her.

She glanced around at the overly large games and their flashing lights. "Well, I don't know. What's yours?"

He glanced at her and grinned. "Let's dance."

Grasping her hand, he pulled her onto the floor set up for *Dance Dance Revolution*. They stood on colored tiles lit from below and the music started. From there they laughed their way through moving their feet to the illuminated squares, like animated twister.

Although she tried to get to yoga or Pilates classes at the gym, work usually kept her too busy to make time for herself. That included having fun. So far in the less than twenty-four hours she'd known Tanner, he'd shown her a good time in more ways than one. She hadn't realized how badly she'd needed to let loose and enjoy until she'd actually engaged herself and forgotten about work.

He had rhythm despite his big, strong body, and she couldn't help but admire the way his jeans molded to his thighs and his burgundy Henley accentuated the muscles in his arms. There were times during their dancing fun that she longed to throw herself into his arms, wrap her legs around his body, and lose herself in him as she'd done last night. But she didn't think the owners would appreciate sex on the dance floor, so she refocused on the games.

They played a variety, from *Guitar Hero* to old-fashioned air hockey and *Mario Kart*, *Skee-Ball*, *Super Shot Basketball*, and more.

By the time they took a break for pizza, she was starving. She sat across from him in a booth in a quiet room and met his blueish-gray gaze.

"Having fun?" he asked.

She nodded. "I had no idea how much I needed a day like this to just relax and have fun. To forget the stress of everyday life and the job." She took a bite of pizza, wiping a bit of sauce off her face.

He leaned in closer and she wanted nothing more than to close the distance and kiss him. All day long, they'd played games, their bodies close, very often him bracketing her against a large gaming station, the feel and scent of him overwhelming her.

"And what is that exactly? What do you do for a living?"

Given how obsessed she was with her career, she was surprised her job hadn't come up before. "Oh! I'm an assistant district attorney."

He blinked, his expression suddenly blank. "An ADA," he said, sounding surprised.

She nodded, taking another bite of pizza. "Yep. Went to law school and everything."

Silence descended on them, taking her by surprise. "Tanner? Are you okay?"

He shook his head, as if coming out of a trance ... or a very serious conversation with himself. "I'm fine." She wasn't sure whether or not to believe him.

"How's the pizza?" he asked, obviously changing the subject.

She looked at him curiously but answered, sensing he didn't want to continue the job conversation any longer. A lot of people had a bias against lawyers, but she hadn't figured he was one of them. "I'm on my third slice. You have to ask?"

He chuckled at her reply and she hoped they'd gone back to normal.

"It's my birthday. I deserve to indulge." She didn't normally eat so much, and she couldn't wait to get home and unbutton her pants.

"Speaking of indulging, I brought the cake pops inside, remember? Do you have room for dessert?"

Holding her stomach, she groaned. "Just one."

He grinned and went to the man who'd greeted them and taken the pops to put aside for him, coming back with a couple of the delicious treats. Just looking at them, suddenly she was hungry again.

"I wish you'd look at me like you're looking at that cake pop," Tanner chuckled as he took a seat beside her. Grasping a pop by the cone, he held it out to her. "Here. Take a bite."

She leaned closer, her eyes on his as she opened her mouth and sank her teeth into the delicious marshmallow pop. "Mmm." She groaned, low in her throat. "God, that's good."

His eyes darkened and he grinned, looking as yummy as the treat. "What's that smile for?" she asked.

"That sound. The last time I heard it, I was deep inside you."

She hadn't expected such a blunt reply and the answer had her tingling inside.

"I want a taste," he murmured, leaning in close.

She wanted the same thing and parted her lips. Next thing she knew, his mouth was on hers. Softly and gently, he licked his way inside. He might be tasting the cake pop but she was indulging in him. The kiss was way too brief when he lifted his head, meeting her gaze.

"Delicious," he said in a gruff voice.

His taste lingered and she agreed. This day had been as special as the man himself.

A little while later, they were in an Uber on the

way to her apartment.

Scarlett lay her head on Tanner's shoulder, overwhelmed in the very best way. Even if she'd celebrated her birthday every year as a child, she couldn't imagine anything better than what he'd given her today.

She sighed.

"What's wrong?" he asked, threading his hand through hers.

"I'm just tired." She wasn't lying but she couldn't share what she'd really been thinking. That would come soon enough.

Because though she'd never had such sexual chemistry with a man, let alone synced on a personal level, Tanner was the one man who could distract her from her goals. And she'd promised her brother, while standing at the cemetery, nobody else would go free and not pay for their crimes if she could help it.

She wasn't looking forward to ending things with him. They'd barely begun and what they had experienced was real, genuine, and fun. But timing everything, and if she looked at her life and the goals she'd laid out for herself, she had no choice.

Chapter Four

AS SCARLETT'S HEAD rested on Tanner's shoulder, nothing had ever felt so right, but he couldn't stop the concerning thoughts circling through his mind.

A district attorney. At her words, everything inside him had frozen. His past, his secrets, the things he was ashamed of were all tied to his acting out and ending up on the wrong side of the law thanks to the temper he worked to keep in check, though it was only directed at people who hurt those he loved. And he knew damn well why he had such an anger issue too. As a kid, he'd felt impotent against the father who used words as a weapon, and he'd been powerless to do anything to stop him from belittling him and his sister. The anger would build and build, but he couldn't direct it at his parent, so he acted out against others who hurt those he cared for.

As she'd spoken, he'd had to do his best to school his features and hide his emotions, not wanting Scarlett to know her career had thrown him for a loop.

Although it sure as hell had reinforced the fact that she was too good for him.

The Uber pulled up to the curb outside her apartment and they exited the vehicle. In silence, he led her to her apartment, his hand on her back.

Once at her door, she turned to face him. "Tanner–"

"Scarlett–" he said at the same time. He shook his head. "You first."

She visibly swallowed hard. "I had such a good time today. I mean, you have no idea what the birthday celebration meant to me and I'll never forget it. But I meant what I said when I told you my job is all consuming. I don't know how to carve out time for a relationship."

Although he hadn't let himself think about where they were going from here, she'd made her position clear this morning. He had pushed for more, had hoped their day together would change her mind. But now that he knew her career, well, he understood they couldn't be more different.

Had he planned to end things? No. Hell, he wasn't even sure what he'd been about to say, but she was giving him an out.

An out he didn't want to take. He brushed her hair off her cheek, stroking her skin with his hand as he did. "I'm going to give you what you want for now. I'll back off."

Meanwhile, he'd take the time to think and re-group. But not before he gave her something to remember him by. Leaning in, he sealed his mouth over hers.

Without hesitating, she parted and let him in, her tongue tangling with his as if they'd been doing this dance *forever*. And as he took his time, sliding his lips over hers, teeth clashing, mouths devouring, one thought went through his mind. He could see himself doing just that.

✧   ✧   ✧

SHAKEN BY THE depth of his feelings and today's revelation, Tanner headed to the club. He didn't want a drink. Since Levi's death, he usually avoided alcohol for himself, which made the fact that he owned the club somewhat ironic. But when they'd decided to open a business and Jason's cousin Gabe had expressed interest in helping them start up what he knew best, the nightclub idea had been born.

Right now he needed to be with the men who understood him best. He passed through the busy club, taking a moment to appreciate what they'd created together before joining his partners in the office on the second floor. He found the guys sitting at their desks, feet propped up, chilling, screens around them showing various sections of the club downstairs.

"Well, look who made it," Jason said, a smug grin on his face. "Where's your girl?"

"Who's my girl is more like it," Tanner muttered, running a hand through his hair.

Just who was the beautiful woman with the amazing laugh who could play video games like a champ, inhale pizza and cake pops, and make him hard at just the thought of her? He still hadn't plumbed the depths of her and he wanted to know more. But could he take the risk of being hurt when she discovered his past?

Jason narrowed his gaze, but before he could question Tanner, Landon spoke. "Am I the only one out of the loop?" Landon asked.

Jason grinned. "Tanner met a woman last night. Took her upstairs. Spent the day with her today. Apparently something happened since to throw you off your game?"

Both men looked to him.

Tanner rolled his shoulders, the movement not easing the tension a damn bit. "She's a fucking assistant district attorney. Not just a lawyer but a prosecutor."

He let the words settle, and each man took the time to put the pieces of Tanner's obvious feelings together.

"So? You're a club owner. Big fucking deal." It

didn't shock Tanner that Jason, the happily settled one of the bunch, could see past the issues inherent in Scarlett's career.

"Your past is your past, Tanner. Let it go," Landon said.

Tanner frowned. He didn't need them both ganging up on him, even if what they said jived with what was in his heart and what he really wanted. Since childhood, he'd been told he wasn't good enough. He'd never make something of himself. He'd nearly proven his father right. It was thanks to these men that he'd pulled himself up from the depths of his despair after Levi's death and the anger that had consumed him. Could he listen to them now?

"What if *she* won't—or can't—live with who I am?" Because in his experience, good girls didn't go for bad guys, and with his record, expunged or not, she deserved better than a guy like him.

"Who you were. And for understandable reasons." Landon, who'd lost his *twin*, strode over and put hand on Tanner's shoulder. "You're not that guy anymore."

"And you'll only know what she can handle if you're honest." Jason eyed him with understanding. "It's not easy to lay it all out there. I know. But it's worth it if she comes around."

"And if she doesn't, she isn't worth it," Landon said.

Jason nodded in agreement.

"I'll think about it."

"Don't think, do," Jason said.

"In other words, don't be a pussy." Landon chuckled and Tanner shot him an annoyed glare.

But the guys had a point. A look at the monitors downstairs showed him what they'd accomplished. How far he'd come. If Scarlett couldn't see him for the man he was… Well, he wouldn't go there. He also had to overcome her resistance to making time for him in her life.

He was up to the challenge. Because he didn't think he could let her go without trying his damndest to see what could be between them. But she'd asked for time and he felt they both needed it.

"Now on to other subjects, any news from the security company or is it time to hire someone else?" Tanner asked.

At the question, Landon strode back to his desk, picked up a sheet of paper, and returned, placing it in front of Tanner. "Bastard was wearing a hoodie and kept his face turned away from the cameras."

"Fuck." Tanner slammed a hand on the desk.

"We're careful. We'll get him," Jason said. "Gabe's pulling his PI in on things. Jack Renault is the best."

"Good," Tanner said with a definitive nod. If Gabriel Dare recommended him, Tanner trusted the man's judgment.

Back when Tanner had gotten himself thrown in jail for assault, Gabe, Jason's cousin, had pulled in favors with some very important people and gotten him an executive pardon and Tanner's convictions went away. It'd been legal, if one counted pulling strings legal. But that was the way of the world. It was all in who one knew.

Tanner had promised everyone they'd never have an issue with him again. And they wouldn't. He'd always hold his temper in check. Therapy and learning about himself assured him of that. Not that he didn't get angry at times, but the fury over Vic, who'd caused Levi's death, was under control because the man was behind bars. And Tanner no longer had a record that would have kept them from opening the club together because he wouldn't have been able to legally get a liquor license. He'd always owe Gabe for what he'd done for him back in the day.

He glanced up at the guys. "We remain vigilant. And meanwhile, we go about business as usual."

✦   ✦   ✦

BEING A LAWYER wasn't all courtroom dramatics like it was on television. It was more about paperwork, research, and more paperwork, interviewing witnesses, and very little sleep. And yet, with as busy as Scarlett had been, she couldn't stop thinking about Tanner. One week had passed since she'd seen him, and though he'd said he'd back off, his qualifier had stayed with her.

For now. He'd back off *for now*. But maybe he'd taken her words at face value, let time pass, and realized she wasn't worth the chase. And really, she'd meant it when she said she didn't have time for a relationship, so why was she so disappointed he'd been MIA?

"Knock knock." Leigh strode into Scarlett's office, carrying a cardboard tray with Starbucks cups in the holders. "Coffee break time," she said and took a seat across from Scarlett's desk.

"That one's yours." Leigh pointed to the cup holding Scarlett's drink.

"A venti," she said with a grateful sigh. "Oh my God, I love you for this." She picked up the cup, pulled out the green stopper, and look a long sip, not caring that it burned her tongue a little. The caffeine more than made up for it as did the steaming taste of caramel.

"If you love me, then talk to me. You've been avoiding the subject of your time with the club hottie all week." Leigh pouted but her hurt was real.

Scarlett sighed. "He was amazing. Like everything I could want in a man ... if I were looking." Leigh opened her mouth to argue but Scarlett finished first. "Which I'm not."

She went on to tell her friend about her birthday weekend and how much Tanner had gone out of his way to make the day special.

"For a smart woman, you're an idiot," Leigh said bluntly. "If a guy treated me so well, I wouldn't be pushing him away."

"You should listen to her." A familiar voice had Scarlett looking away from Leigh and up to the doorway, where Tanner stood, arms folded across his chest, a sexy grin on his face.

"How did you get past Michelle out front?" Scarlett asked, noting that Leigh had jumped to her feet and began fixing her dress and smoothing out the wrinkles.

She held back a grin. Tanner had that effect on women. They wanted to look their best. She, on the other hand, refused to think about the fact that it was three p.m., her makeup had long since faded, her hair was up in a bun, and since it wasn't court day, she was in an unmemorable pair of pinstriped pants and a pink shirt.

"There was no one at the desk out front so I walked in, asked someone where your office was, and here I am." He leaned against the doorframe, a hot guy in black slacks and a long-sleeve plum-colored dress shirt.

"Hi, I'm Leigh Michaels," she said, extending her hand, and Tanner took it.

"Tanner Grayson. And I appreciate you pushing Scarlett in my direction."

"Have any friends just like you?" Leigh asked.

Tanner chuckled and Scarlett rolled her eyes. "Leigh brought me Starbucks and she was just leaving."

"Nice to meet you, Leigh."

"Bye." She smiled at him, turned to Scarlett and winked, and walked out of the office, leaving her alone with Tanner.

"She's…"

"Something," Scarlett filled in the word Tanner hadn't yet said. "But she's a good friend." She met his gaze. "What are you doing here?"

"I tried to do what you wanted. To stay away." He hesitated before speaking. "I missed you," he said, shutting the door behind him.

She swallowed hard. "I missed you too. But nothing in my life has changed." She gestured to the mountains of files surrounding her desk and cardboard boxes filled with the same piled on the floor. Discovery. All the evidence in her current case there for her to scour through.

"I'm not asking to take over your life. Just for you

to carve out a small part. Unless what we shared was normal to you? Could you find our kind of chemistry and fun with just anyone else?" The smug smirk on his face told her he already knew the answer.

"Dinners fit in between work. An occasional couple of hours on the weekends. You're willing to put up with that? Because in my experience…" She paused because he stalked toward her, coming around the desk and bracing his hands on the arms of her chair.

"Yes? Tell me about your experience before me." A hint of mint on his breath combined with his musky cologne, making for a potent combination.

Her breath hitched and her body responded, swaying toward him. "My last… The last guy who said no problem gave up on me."

Tanner's gaze narrowed. "He wasn't me. And he sounds like an idiot."

She couldn't stop the smile that hit her lips.

"And that's the last I want to hear of any exes when I'm with you." He straightened and looked at her, his expression serious. "But there are things you need to know about me before we move forward."

Her cell phone rang and her father's name came up on the screen. She shot Tanner a regret-filled look. "I have to take this."

He stepped back and she felt the loss of his warmth.

"Dad?"

Her father rambled nearly incoherent. "Is Colleen there?" she asked.

All Scarlett could hear was something about an emergency and the nurse leaving. She picked up other bits and pieces that had her utterly petrified. "Where are you?"

"The hospital with your mother," he finally said clearly.

Her heart nearly stopped. "What hospital?"

Tanner froze, his concerned gaze on hers.

"Okay, yes. Yes. I'm coming." She disconnected the call, her hands shaking. "I need to tell my boss I have to go." She picked up the landline and dialed. "Kyle? I have a family emergency. I need to leave for the day and I'm not sure about tomorrow." She stood up, already throwing her cell into her purse. "I know what I have to do but my mother's in the hospital. I'm leaving." She disconnected the call and looked at Tanner, who stood waiting patiently.

"What hospital?" he asked gently.

"North Shore. In Manhasset." Realizing she'd put her phone in her bag and she needed it to call for an Uber, she started to search her large bag. Somehow between the time she'd tossed it in and now, it had gotten lost in her mess.

"Scarlett, calm down. I've got it," he said, his

phone in his hand, the Uber app pulled up on his screen. "Come on."

She let him walk her to the elevator and hit the lobby button, her father's words starting to make sense. Colleen had gotten an emergency call from her daughter, who was in early labor, and she had to leave. Her father said it was fine and he'd be home soon. He arrived home to find her mother in the extra car in the garage with the motor running, the garage door closed.

A car pulled up to the front of Scarlett's work building, and Tanner leaned down to the passenger window. "Tanner Grayson?" the driver asked.

Nodding, Tanner opened the back door so Scarlett could slide in. To her shock, he climbed in after her, slamming the door shut behind them. "North Shore Hospital," he confirmed with the driver.

"Wait, what are you doing?"

"Going with you," he said, pulling her tight against him as the car sped off. "Now what happened?"

Too stunned and frightened to argue, she told him what she'd put together. "My mother tried to kill herself," she whispered. "Carbon monoxide poisoning." She swallowed hard. "I told you already she has severe depressive disorder, but she's never tried anything like this before."

He cupped her face in his hands. "I'm sorry, honey. Are you okay?"

She swallowed hard. "I'm trying. Dad was incoherent and I don't know anything, which makes it harder. I don't know if she was unconscious or if he found her in time..." She began to tremble and he pulled her into his arms, letting her cry.

She needed the release before she arrived at the hospital. Someone had to be strong and coherent to understand what the doctors said. To make decisions. And her father hadn't sounded like he'd be in any shape to handle things.

She slipped her hand into Tanner's, grateful for his presence. They hadn't known each other long, but it felt natural to rely on him for support. She didn't have time to sort out her feelings for him now, but they were growing. Quickly.

TANNER HAD GONE to talk to Scarlett to confess his past sins and see if they stood a chance. Instead he had a crying woman in his arms and was on his way to the hospital with no idea what they'd find out when they arrived.

"Do you have tissues in your purse?" he asked.

She lifted her head, sniffed, and nodded. She pulled one out. He took it and softly wiped under her eyes, catching tears and makeup.

She looked at him curiously. "Deal with a lot of

crying women?"

"I have a sister," he explained.

She nodded. "Tell me about her."

He knew the underlying sentiment. Take her mind off the unknown. He didn't mind talking about his sibling. "So Alyssa is older than me by four years. She planned to go to school to become a nurse but life had other plans. She got pregnant after her college graduation."

"She couldn't do both? I know it's hard but–"

"My father's a bastard," he found himself saying. Now that he hadn't anticipated discussing. "He was a real bully while we were growing up but he mostly aimed it at me."

She turned to face him, her expression soft and understanding. "Go on."

"But when Alyssa turned up pregnant, he wouldn't let my mother help her, and what Don Grayson says goes, at least in his home." He swallowed hard. "I wasn't in any position at that point to help, and Nick Dobbins, the guy who got her pregnant, stepped up. He's a mechanic and he wanted to marry her and take care of her and the baby. They have a son, by the way. His name is Cal and he's a great kid."

"I love the smile on your face when you talk about him," she said.

He chuckled. "He's a teenager and he alternates

between being a big goofball and trying to be the adult he isn't ready to be." He shook his head, laughing. "But back to Alyssa's story, they couldn't afford daycare if she went back for her nursing degree so … she made a sacrifice but she's happy now."

"That's… Well, I don't know what to say really. I'm sorry she missed out on the career she wanted but glad she has a family she loves."

"Exactly how I feel. Except I hate my father for not being there for her when she needed her parents the most. Hell, I hated him anyway," he said, feeling his hands curl into fists and immediately releasing the tension before Scarlett could notice.

"I wish you'd had it better growing up," she murmured, her soft hand cupping his cheek. "You deserved better. You and your sister, both. You already know my childhood story." At the memory, she stiffened, the reminder of where they were headed suddenly front and center once more.

Luckily there hadn't been much traffic and the car pulled up in front of the emergency room, and they exited the vehicle. He let her take the lead, his hand on her back so she knew she wasn't dealing with things alone.

Scarlett gave her mother's name at the desk and a woman directed them around the corner, down a long hall, to the waiting room.

As soon as they walked through the doors, Scarlett called out, "Dad!" and ran into her father's arms.

Tanner took a slow walk over, giving them a few seconds together before he joined them.

She stepped back, her eyes red as she met his gaze. "Dad, this is Tanner Grayson. He brought me here. Tanner, this is my father, Mack."

Tanner shook the man's hand. One look and he saw the father-daughter resemblance, the sandy-blond hair and the green eyes.

"They have her in a hyperbaric oxygen chamber," Mack said, wringing his hands. "Apparently oxygen is the treatment for this kind of thing but the basic inhalation isn't working. This is one of the few hospitals that has the chamber, and when she wouldn't come around with oxygen the regular way, they resorted to using it."

Scarlett nodded, and though Tanner wanted to haul her into his arms, he couldn't make a scene.

"What do the doctors know?" she asked.

Mack ran a hand through his already wild hair. "Not much. At least not yet. It's my fault. I told Colleen she could leave. I rushed right home. I was at a call nearby and I went right home. She couldn't have been in that car with the engine running for more than five minutes."

"That's all it takes," Scarlett said, grabbing her father's shaking hands. "It's not your fault. It's a symptom of her depression. You had to let Colleen go to her daughter." She drew a deep breath. "When will we know something?"

"The doctor said he'd update me periodically."

"Can I get you coffee? Food? Something to drink?" Tanner offered them both.

They shook their heads in unison.

The three of them sat down and time ticked by slowly. Occasionally one would get up, pace, sit down again. Then someone else would begin. Tanner called the guys and explained why he wouldn't be at the club tonight, despite Scarlett insisting he should go. He wasn't leaving her alone.

He knew what it was like to worry about a loved one. Maybe not a parent but Levi. He'd sat in the ER after they'd carried him, unconscious, out of that fucking frat house, walking until a campus van picked them up on the road. He'd been DOA but none of them knew for sure. They'd waited and waited in a room just like this one for news. So he wasn't leaving her.

An hour and a half after they'd arrived, a man in a white coat walked into the room. "Davis? The Davis family?"

Scarlett and her father jumped out of their seats.

"She's awake," he said and Tanner flew out of his

seat, getting his arms around Scarlett before her knees buckled. She felt so fragile in his arms.

"Thank God," she said, her voice cracking.

"When can we see her?" Mack asked.

"I'd like to talk to you first."

Scarlett leaned into him. "Go on," she said to the doctor.

The balding man gave her a nod. "We're going to keep her overnight. Run some tests, make sure there's no damage that we can assess right away. But I've spoken with Mrs. Davis's psychiatrist and we are in agreement that she's a danger to herself, and with her years of treatment-resistant depression, we believe she belongs in a residential psychiatric facility at this time."

"I tried so hard at home but it's become so difficult. Beyond what I can do. I—" Mack's voice shook with emotion.

"It's doing the best thing for your wife, Mr. Davis," the doctor said.

Mack nodded.

Scarlett's eyes glistened with tears.

But as Tanner glanced from father to daughter, they looked … relieved, something he could understand. Her mother would be under constant supervision. She couldn't hurt herself.

"A social worker will be by to help you with paperwork." The doctor placed a hand on Mack's shoulder. "As soon as she's settled in a room, we'll let you see her."

"Thank you," Scarlett and Mack said at the same time.

Hours later, Scarlett had seen her still-nonresponsive mother. Tanner had seen her at her weakest and at her strongest. Watching her handle her personal crisis made him fall for her even more. She didn't *need* him but he knew she appreciated his presence, and he was happy to be able to give her his strength when hers failed.

With exhaustion seeping in, Scarlett and Tanner settled Mack in an Uber since he'd accompanied the ambulance to the hospital. And their own car picked them up to go back to the city.

"God, I'm beat." Scarlett yawned, then met his gaze. "Thank you. I don't know why you stuck it out all night. Want to explain?"

"First, don't thank me, okay?" He didn't want her to feel obligated to him in any way.

She nodded, her eyes on his.

"Second, I stayed because I care. And because I understand what you're going through. Well, sort of." Levi once again came to mind.

"How–"

Tanner placed a finger over her lips. "No questions tonight, okay? We can crash and deal with everything else in the morning."

She exhaled a long breath. "Sounds good. Can we drop you off first?" she offered.

He grinned at her. "When I said *we can crash*, I meant *we* can crash. Together. Somehow I think you just need to be held tonight. And I know I need to hold you."

And when they finally did fall into bed together, Scarlett passed out immediately but Tanner lay awake thinking. He still hadn't told her his secrets but he'd fallen harder for the prosecutor. And if she had walls up before she knew his truths, what would she do once she found out?

Chapter Five

S CARLETT WOKE UP in her own bed with unfamiliar heat bracketing her body. Yesterday's events came back to her immediately—her mother trying to kill herself and the man who was currently wrapped around her, who'd had her back every step of the way. Not ready to face the day, she closed her eyes and sighed.

"Are you up?" Tanner asked from behind her.

"I don't want to be."

He squeezed her tighter. "How about you call your dad and reassure yourself your mom is okay?"

She nodded and reached for her cell on the nightstand. A few minutes later, she'd spoken to her father, who was calmer and in a much better mental state than last night.

She disconnected the call and put the phone back on the nightstand before rolling to face Tanner. "Mom had a peaceful night." Scarlett had relaxed after finding that out.

"Are you going to go over to the hospital today?"

he asked.

She met his gaze. "I don't know. Dad says he's meeting with the social worker this morning, and he seems to have things under control. As much as I hate to admit it, I think a treatment facility is the best place for her."

Tanner nodded in understanding. "I got that feeling from both of you last night. I'm sure it's exhausting worrying about your mother all the time. And your father has done all he can at home."

The familiar lump rose in her throat along with tears floating in her eyes. "It's sad. And frustrating. Sometimes I'm angry that she won't just snap out of it even though I know she can't control it. Mental illness is no different than any physical one that needs treatment. Either a person responds to it or they don't."

He tucked her hair behind her ear. "Well, she has a good family and support, and maybe your dad needs a break. This solution will give him one."

She nodded. "I hope insurance covers things." She knew her father had a good medical plan but not extra money to keep her mother in a facility indefinitely.

"And that's why the social worker gets involved. You said your dad has things handled. Why don't you take the day off and give yourself a chance to accept and process things. If you decide you want to head over to the hospital later, we can do that."

"But work—"

He shook his head. "You already told your boss you didn't know if you'd be in today. Cut yourself some slack. This is a legitimate personal family emergency."

His words made sense and she needed the space from both the pressures of the office and the ones at home. She relaxed on her side, her head against the pillow, staring into his eyes. "You're persuasive, Mr. Grayson."

He tapped her nose and grinned. "I just know what you need."

"What's that?"

He pulled her close. "You need me." He kissed her mouth. "Inside you." He licked his tongue over her lips. "Now."

She wasn't about to argue with something that could make her feel good when she needed it.

His hands trailed down her sides and her nipples puckered at the sensual way his fingertips glided over her skin.

"I want you naked." He lifted her nightshirt up and over her head, baring her top half.

She immediately wriggled out of her panties and kicked them to the side. "Condom?" she asked.

He reached over for his jeans on the floor, pulling

one out of his pocket.

She eyed him with a knowing grin.

In an instant, he'd shucked the boxer briefs he'd slept in and rose over her. She parted her legs and he slid into the space she made for him, his hard erection nudging against her sex. She moaned at the feel of him parting her and thrusting inside. He filled her, thick and pulsing, until thoughts of anything but him disappeared.

Spearing her hands into his hair, she held on as he pumped his hips back and forth, gliding into her, groaning as he bottomed out inside. "Damn. It's like you were made for me."

Her lips parted and he took advantage, sealing his mouth over hers. He kissed her hard and fucked her harder, his tongue perfectly mimicking the thrust of his hips and the way he consumed her. He pumped in and out and she closed her eyes, savoring the determined way he took her.

So she was surprised when he slid out of her, leaving her empty. "What...?"

He met her gaze, eyes gleaming with desire as he moved off her. "Hands and knees," he instructed in a sexy growl.

She didn't hesitate to do as he said, shifting onto her stomach and raising herself up, ass in the air. He came over her in an instant, his thick cock once again aligned at her entrance. He gripped her hip with one hand, and as he entered her, a low, sexy noise rumbled in his throat.

He felt bigger this way, thicker inside her, and her inner walls began to ripple around him, pulses of desire that felt incredible. "Tanner," she moaned.

He gathered her hair in his hand and pulled it to the side. "Say my name again and I might come from the sound alone," he said, his breath warm in her ear, the heat of his body at her back.

"Tanner," she repeated, unable to resist teasing him.

He tightened his grip and began to take her with a hard thrusting of his hips, his thighs slapping against hers.

"Oh, God. That feels so good."

"I can make it better." He reached around her waist and slid a finger over her clit, causing waves of pleasure to build again. His hard cock pummeled her from the inside and his finger brought her higher on the outside. She pushed back, meeting him thrust for thrust, her entire being focused on one thing only. "I need to come," she said, trembling uncontrollably beneath him, her body on the verge of exploding.

He pinched her clit.

It was all she needed for her body to let loose, and everything coalesced as she came hard, her orgasm overtaking her, waves of pleasure consuming her.

Her climax triggered something primal in him and he began to thrust harder. She hadn't thought it was possible but he slammed into her with a punishing rhythm that set off another orgasm inside of her at the same moment he came with a shout, stilling as his orgasm gripped him. He clutched her waist possessively as he collapsed on top of her and she fell to the mattress, completely fulfilled.

Later, after they'd showered and ordered in something to eat because her refrigerator was empty, she looked at him across the table. "I need to go see my mother." She'd been debating for a while now and decided she couldn't live with herself if she didn't go visit again today.

He nodded as if he'd expected her words. "I know. I just wanted you to have a break before you needed to deal with reality again."

She propped her chin in her hand and met his gaze. His hair was rumpled from her hands pulling at the longer strands and his eyes held a warmth she sensed he didn't give to most people. A far cry from the man who'd come down on the elevator and surveyed his domain, she mused. She didn't want to let him down but she had a feeling sooner or later, she would. He'd grow tired of her being busy all the time.

And speaking of busy ... she rose to her feet. "I

should get ready."

He nodded, standing too. "And I have to be at the club for a meeting with the guys before opening." He held out one hand. "Now say goodbye the right way."

She was getting used to his bossy ways and stepped into the crook of his arm, tipping her head up for the kiss he'd all but demanded. He deserved one.

After all, he'd given her exactly what she needed. Not that sex had been a hardship for him, she mused, but it was the fact that he'd known how to soothe her ragged edges that stayed with her long after he'd put her in an Uber to go deal with her family alone.

IT TOOK EVERYTHING inside Tanner not to head over to the hospital with Scarlett again, but they weren't at that point where he should be with her twenty-four seven. More importantly, she needed to see that she could live her life and he'd keep showing up, being there, not running off like the last loser she'd dated.

Which was why he'd let the last week go by, allowing a slow get-to-know-you period, when all he wanted was to barrel his way into her life and make her his. If asked, Tanner wouldn't have said he believed in love at first sight, but from the second he'd stepped off the elevator and met Scarlett's gaze, he'd known she was different. That he had to have her.

And after spending time with her both in bed and out, he understood he wouldn't be letting her go. Of course, he might not have a say in the matter. She still didn't know about his past. After her mother's suicide attempt had taken precedence over his confession, he'd decided to let her get to know and trust him before he dumped his shit in her lap and discovered whether she'd go running. He knew Scarlett was a strong woman and could handle his old issues. The question was whether or not she'd want to.

In the meantime, he'd learned all the restaurants around the area of her office and had gotten in the habit of bringing her lunch so they could hang out and talk while they ate. True, he was stealing an hour of her time because, prior to him, Scarlett worked through lunch, but after the third day, she'd stopped complaining. After the first week, she'd begun to text him what she wanted to eat instead of making him guess—in the incorrect assumption he'd give up and not come by at all.

This morning, he'd woken up early and worked out at the gym, sparring with a partner before showering there. He expected to receive a lunch text with her daily meal request but his phone screen was empty.

He frowned and texted her. No quick reply. If she'd had to be in court, she'd have let him know not to plan on coming for lunch. Frowning, he pulled up the Uber app and put in her office address. Though he tried to call her on the drive over, she didn't answer.

He worried something had happened with her mother, but he knew Maxine was in a good facility, and though she wasn't making progress, she couldn't hurt herself either.

He took the elevator to Scarlett's work floor, waved at Michelle at reception, who by now he'd met. She just grinned and watched as he walked past. Considering she didn't stop him, he knew Scarlett was in her office. Maybe she'd gotten so busy she'd just forgotten to text him.

Her door was closed and he knocked. She didn't answer. He knocked again and let himself in.

Scarlett sat at her desk, a photograph in her hand, tears in her eyes.

"Hey. What's wrong?" he asked, coming up to her. He glanced down and saw the picture of her brother, the one she kept on the windowsill.

"It's an anniversary of a really bad day." She looked up at him, her gaze glassy with unshed tears.

He settled on the edge of her desk but didn't take the picture from her hand. He remembered her telling him her brother had died. He knew from experience what that date could mean to the people who loved the deceased person.

"Tell me what happened."

She put the photo against her chest. "He was working at a bodega near our apartment. A small convenience store. And a group of guys came in and held up the place. Hank, my brother ... he..." She swallowed hard. "He didn't want to give them the money in the register. You see, he knew that Mr. Sawyer, the owner, needed every penny for his wife's asthma treatments. "They shot him in cold blood."

He closed his eyes briefly, then opened them again. "I'm sorry."

She nodded. "Thank you. Me too."

He pried the picture from her clutches and set it back on the shelf where she normally kept it. Looking over her.

Then he took her hands. "I understand, you know. Landon, his twin, Levi, Jason, and I met in college. Manhattan University. We were freshmen and imme-diate best friends. Levi wanted to join a frat. My gut screamed it was a bad idea. Hell, none of us wanted it except Levi. But he was bold and brash and kind of our pack leader. So he convinced us."

She listened, her gaze never leaving his.

"The guys who ran the frat were assholes. One in particular, Victor Clark." He forced air into his lungs as he said the name, did the deep breathing his thera-pist had recommended in order to control the anger that came over him when Vic's name came up.

"There was hazing, despite school rules against it, but until then, nothing we couldn't handle. But the night of the final initiation, we'd heard rumors the party got out of control. We shouldn't have gone…" He shook his head. "The drinking was over-the-top. Shots, drinks, paddling, pain … and then we were each given a handle of what we thought was regular vodka."

"It wasn't?" she asked.

Tanner shook his head. "Turns out it was one hundred proof but we didn't know it at the time. And Levi volunteered to go first. We begged him to leave." He remembered his gut screaming at him. "Landon said fuck the frat. But Levi wouldn't listen. He drank. Vic handed him a backpack filled with rocks. Made him run up and down the stairs… He tripped, Vic slapped him, told him to keep going. Levi tried, fell backward…"

If Tanner told the rest, he'd throw up. His friend's head banging on the stairs. The blood on the floor, Landon hitting his brother's face, begging him to wake up.

"Jesus, Tanner. I'm sorry," Scarlett said, her voice cracking.

He managed a grim smile. "The club is named after the date he died. So I really do understand what today means to you."

She squeezed his hand. "Sucks to have the death

of a loved one in common."

He blew out a long breath, realizing they'd just shared something heavy. "Your brother would be proud of you." Hell, Tanner was proud of her and he'd just begun to scratch the surface.

"I hope so." Scarlett glanced at the picture, then up at Tanner. "The guys who robbed the store and killed Hank, their lawyer got their case thrown out on a technicality." Her eyes burned with anger, her entire body vibrating with it. "They walked free and that's when I decided to become a lawyer. To make sure that no one who committed a crime would get away with it easily, not if I could help it."

Tanner stilled. "That's ... good," he managed to say. Even as his heart squeezed tighter inside his chest. His past not only included being arrested for assault but for skating on it after Gabriel Dare pulled strings. He didn't think that was something Scarlett would understand or forgive.

Which meant they'd gone from something that bonded them to something else that could tear them apart. He had a record. She put away criminals. He'd had his record expunged. She resented people who got away with crimes no matter how they'd done it.

"I need to go." He pushed himself up from her desk.

"Tanner?"

"I forgot about a security meeting at the club," he lied.

"What?" Scarlett stood up, obviously surprised. "Are you okay? I know we just talked about some pretty deep stuff."

He clenched his jaw, only knowing that he needed space. He had to take a big step back from Scarlett, because everything that defined him was everything this woman despised.

HOURS LATER, IN the late evening, Tanner picked up his cell phone, pulled up Scarlett's name … and put it down on his desk again. "You're an asshole," he muttered to himself, still annoyed he'd walked out on her earlier today.

But as soon as he'd heard the venom in her tone as she'd described why she'd become an attorney and how she'd never accept someone getting off for a crime without paying, he knew he'd probably lost her before he'd ever truly had her.

"Finally realizing what we all know?" Jason asked, striding into the office and sitting down in a chair across from Tanner.

The main office they shared consisted of desks for all three men along with a couch and chair area where they sat now. Chrome and glass desks along with black and chrome chairs, a look similar to the club itself, made up the décor. Sleek and elegant, as Gabe and his decorator sister, Lucy, had recommended.

"Funny." Frowning, he glanced at his phone once more. "What are you doing here? I thought you and Landon were downstairs."

All three of them were at the club tonight. Faith had a party she'd created candy party favors for, and she'd been asked to stay and hand them out, which left Jason at loose ends. And here at work.

"Landon was worried about you. He said you were upstairs moping and that, since I was attached by a ball and chain, maybe I could understand." Jason shrugged, clearly unaffected by Landon's words about his marriage.

Ever since he'd gotten together with Faith, it was like a huge burden and shadow of pain had been lifted from Jason's shoulders. Landon was happy for Jason. He just couldn't understand the feelings that his friend experienced … and neither had Tanner. Until he met Scarlett.

"So Landon's the asshole."

Jason narrowed his gaze. "No changing the subject. How did you fuck up with Scarlett and can I help?"

Tanner ran a hand over his face, about to explain when both of their phones began to buzz at the same time. Alarmed, they both grabbed for their cells.

"Yeah?" Tanner asked.

"Someone called in a bomb threat. We're evacuating," Landon said.

Tanner had no doubt Landon was getting the same call from security. They both jumped up from their chairs and headed downstairs, unsure of what to expect or whether or not it was a credible threat.

✧　✧　✧

"I DON'T UNDERSTAND it, Leigh. One minute he was sitting here listening to me pour my heart out and him doing the same, and the next he couldn't leave fast enough." Scarlett sat in her office, hours after Tanner had abruptly walked out, and she still had no better comprehension of what had occurred.

"You said he told you something personal, right? Maybe he just couldn't handle talking about it."

Scarlett nodded. "Maybe. I told him about Hank, he reciprocated about Levi, something spooked him, and he left." She played with her bracelet, which she'd had fixed as soon as possible after Tanner had returned it.

"Look into his background," Leigh suggested.

Scarlett whipped her head up to meet her friend's gaze. "What? No. He told me what I needed to know." Exposing herself to another person didn't come easily to Scarlett, so she didn't hold it against Tanner that he hadn't found it easy either.

But he'd seen her family drama firsthand. She'd confided in him about Hank. Why had he felt the need to take off?

"Come on, Scarlett. You told me his best friend died in a hazing incident in college. That's not a typical thing to happen. Don't you want more details?" Leigh crossed her legs in front of her, staring Scarlett down. "I'm certain the information is available online."

"No." Scarlett had already done her own surface search. He'd told her enough.

Besides, after Tanner's departure, she'd finally gone onto Club TEN29's website and scrolled around, coming to the About page regarding the three partners. Full-color photos of each man greeted her, and though she hadn't met the other guys in person, they were all good-looking, though none had the rougher appearance that Tanner had, the darker look in his eyes that drew her to him.

She'd scrolled to a dedication that brought tears to her eyes now that she knew the whole story. *Club TEN29 is named in memory of Levi Bennett, who died in a tragic accident on October 29, 2009*, beneath the photograph of a young man who appeared almost identical to the older photo of Landon.

She swallowed hard. "I'm not going to go digging any further. He'll tell me more if he wants to confide in me. Besides, I doubt I'd find anything that would explain his behavior."

Leigh pulled her phone out of her pants pocket. "Fine. If you're not curious, I am. A few taps of my finger…" She typed something into her browser and wrinkled her nose as she scrolled down the screen. "Aha. Hazing death at Manhattan U involving four freshmen. Tanner's name is here."

"Cut it out, Leigh. I need to get back to work."

"Fine. But if he were my guy, I'd run a background check. Just saying." She shrugged her shoulders, gave one last glance at the screen, and laid it down on her lap.

Scarlett braced her hands on the desk and stared at her friend. "You checked out Cliff?" she asked of the man Leigh was now steadily seeing, horrified at the prospect.

"Damn right I did. I need to make sure the man's record is clean and there's no wife I don't know about."

She shook her head. "You've got trust issues, my friend."

Leigh flushed but she didn't back down. "I'm just saving myself a lot of trouble. Why fall hard for a guy if he's only going to turn out to be someone you can't be with for whatever reason? Better to know sooner rather than later."

"Go away," Scarlett moaned, laying her head in her

hands. If Tanner needed space, she'd give him space. It wasn't like they had a commitment or anything. But the stricken look on his face had stayed with her as did the twisting in her stomach when he'd left so abruptly.

For someone who claimed not to have the time or desire for a relationship, she was certainly letting him work his way into her life ... and her heart. As it was, she'd had to work late tonight to make up for all the frustrated daydreaming and wondering she'd done all afternoon. Not to mention the morning she'd lost remembering Hank. Leigh had a big robbery case and she'd stayed late as well, which had brought her to Scarlett's office for a break. This was their schedule, their lives.

"Hey. Just heard about a bomb scare downtown on the news." Paul Schaffer, a fellow ADA stuck his head into Scarlett's office. Another late-night worker.

"Really? Where?" Leigh asked, rising as did Scarlett so they could follow Paul back to the conference room, where there was a large-screen television bolted to the wall.

Scarlett stepped into the room, immediately catching sight of the reporter on the scene. But it was the location of the bomb scare that had her freezing in her tracks.

"Club TEN29." She pulled on Leigh's hand. "It's Tanner's club. I have to go."

Chapter Six

BY THE TIME Scarlett and Leigh arrived on scene – they'd had to get dropped off far from the site and show credentials to get past barricades—the club had been emptied out and the police were talking to as many people as they could to see if anyone had seen anything of interest.

She looked around, wanting to see Tanner. Although she knew there'd been no blast, the entire incident had frightened her and she needed to see for herself that he was okay.

"I see someone I know. I'm going to try to find out what's going on," Leigh said, placing a hand on Scarlett's arm. "Are you okay?"

She nodded. "I'm going to look for Tanner."

"Okay, I have my cell. Text me and I'll do the same." Leigh pulled her in for a reassuring hug before heading over to a woman Scarlett had never seen before.

Blowing out a deep breath, Scarlett walked around, searching for Tanner or one of his partners, coming up empty.

"Scarlett!"

She turned at the sound of her name. An officer she recognized from some of the crime scenes she worked called her over and she headed his way. "Hi, Frank. What's going on here?"

Officer Frank Rhodes scowled as he turned toward the club. "Apparently more than we knew about. They've been having some vandalism issues they didn't report. Now a bomb scare."

She blinked in surprise. Clearly the police weren't the only ones Tanner hadn't told of his business issues. He'd never mentioned to her that there were problems at the club. "Was the scare legitimate? Did they find anything?"

"Not so far," he said with a shake of his head. "Doesn't appear to be a credible threat. Just one aimed at hurting their business. Asshole owners thought they could handle it themselves." He jerked his head and Scarlett glanced in that direction.

Tanner stood with his partners in an alley beside the club, all three men looking pissed off. He caught her gaze, his eyes opening wide at the sight of her, then warming as he reassured her with a wink.

"Thank God," she murmured under her breath.

"You involved with him?" Frank, who Scarlett knew from work and past crime scenes, not as a friend, asked.

She stiffened at the sound of his judgmental tone. "Who?"

"Grayson."

"I don't see how that's any of your business." She pulled her suit jacket around her and met his gaze.

"Whoa." Frank held up his hands. "Just trying to do you a favor. You seem like a classy woman who can do better than a lowlife like him."

Scarlett narrowed her gaze. "Just what do you think you know about Tanner?"

He let out a rough laugh. "Grew up in the same neighborhood. The guy likes to use his fists. Got himself tossed out of his fancy college and eventually ended up behind bars for assault. Then his partner's rich cousin bailed him out, pulled some strings, and got his record expunged."

She stilled, taking in the information. "He what?" she asked, but she'd heard. Oh, she had heard.

The man she was falling for had been arrested for beating someone up and had gotten himself off. Just like her brother's killers.

"I gotta go talk to more club patrons. Just be careful." Frank walked away, leaving her off-kilter. Clearly Frank had some sort of grudge with Tanner, but his information, if true, was disturbing.

Scarlett wasn't the type of person to judge someone by facts she'd been told secondhand, but she didn't like hearing that anyone had gotten away with something thanks to favors pulled—any more than a person walking on a technicality. Which was how her brother's killers had gone free.

She swallowed hard, needing to process what she'd heard. Decide how she felt about it. Whether it changed her burgeoning feelings for Tanner.

She looked his way but he and his partners had disappeared. She ran her tongue over her lips, knowing they needed to talk. But it wouldn't be happening tonight.

Time to get an Uber, she thought. She opened her phone and texted Leigh, who said she'd meet her at the curb. She was about to head there when she had the distinct sense of being watched.

She glanced up into a pair of glittering eyes, staring at her and taking her in, the man's leering gaze trailing over her from head to toe. A slick smile crossed his face and he drew a line across his throat.

Her eyes opened wide just as Leigh joined her. "What's wrong? You look pale."

"Frank!" She glanced around frantically. "Frank!"

The cop came rushing to her. "What's wrong?"

"That man—" She turned to point where she'd seen him but he was gone. Shaking, she wrapped her arms around herself. "Never mind." She swallowed hard.

"There was a guy who freaked me out but he's gone."

"Office Rhodes, ass over here," someone yelled.

"I'm sorry. If you're okay?" She nodded and he headed to talk to his superior.

"Scarlett?" Leigh asked, obviously worried.

"I'm fine. Just get me out of here."

Leigh glanced around. "This is our car. I called."

"Leigh?" a female driver asked through the open window.

Scarlett let out a relieved breath and nodded. "Yes. Thank you." She quickly opened the door and slid into the car and Leigh followed, slamming the door and locking it behind her.

Leaning against the back seat, Scarlett groaned, happy to be safely enclosed in the car and on her way home.

HOURS LATER, TANNER and his partners sat in their office, trying to come to terms with how serious shit had gotten around them. If Sutherland wanted to make his point, he'd fucking made it.

Tanner had been sucker-punched twice. Standing with Jason and Landon when his gaze had fallen on Scarlett. Seeing she'd come to check on him, relief had filled him … and then he'd laid eyes on her talking to Frank Rhodes, the asshole from his childhood. And before he could process *that*, he'd seen Vic. Larger than life and out of jail.

Anger like he hadn't felt in years had boiled inside Tanner, and it'd taken Landon and Jason holding him back from beating the living daylights out of the man. They'd literally dragged him inside before he could cause damage, not just to Vic – nobody gave a shit about Vic – but to himself and the guys. And, he realized now, to Scarlett, who would have seen the whole thing.

He unbuttoned the top buttons on shirt, which were strangling him, and threw his jacket onto the floor. "How the fuck did he get out of jail?" he asked, pacing the room.

"No idea." Landon shoved his hands into his pants pockets, his jaw working overtime. "But we can't let him destroy everything we've worked for."

"Which is why you should have let me go after him instead of dragging my ass inside." Tanner kicked the nearest thing to him, the trash can in the office. It spilled over, contents with it.

"And that's why we're in here and you're not beating Vic until he's bloody and unconscious. Then we lose you to the system and we're not fucking having it. Got it?" Jason asked him.

He stood in Tanner's face, unafraid of his temper because everyone understood Tanner's anger was never ever directed at those he cared about. Only those who hurt him in ways he never overcame. Victor Clark was about the only person who could work him into that kind of rage these days.

"Fuck." He knew Jason was right.

He also realized his friends hadn't mentioned potentially losing the club. They weren't worried about the business, they were worried about him. And he needed to get himself together so he didn't let them down. Vic pushed his buttons like nobody's business. But he had to learn to keep that demon in check, especially if the bastard was out of jail.

He blew out a long breath and sat down in his seat. "I'm fine. You don't need to worry."

"Did I see Scarlett here?" Jason asked.

Tanner swallowed hard. "She was talking to Frank Rhodes. We grew up in the same neighborhood but now he's a cop," Tanner muttered. "Guy's a prick. Always had it in for me. I liked a girl? He went after her. Just an all-around dick." And the things he could tell her about him? Before he had a chance?

Damn.

"Maybe he was questioning her?" Landon suggested. "Like he thought she was in the club when the bomb threat came in?"

Tanner shook his head. "It looked like they were acquaintances. And Frank knows all my secrets.

Everything we buried."

"It's not like we killed someone. Those secrets can't destroy you."

He swallowed hard. "But given what I learned today, they can cost me Scarlett." He ran a hand through his hair. "Her brother was killed in a convenience store robbery and the assholes got off on a technicality. She's made it her mission to not let people work the system. Like we did for me."

"It was a legal way of going about things," Jason reminded him. "An executive pardon. You went through a bad time after Levi died. We all did. You did your community service. You have no record. If Scarlett can't forgive your past…"

"She doesn't deserve me. Yeah, yeah." He drew a deep breath. "I'll talk to her. And I'll also have her find out how the hell Vic got out of prison."

The sound of a throat clearing interrupted them. "Excuse me." The cop in charge of the bomb threat investigation stood in the office doorway, Rhodes by his side.

"Yes. What can we do for you?" Jason asked.

Tanner watched Frank warily.

"I just wanted to let you know we're finished for tonight. If you need us, give the station a call. Otherwise we'll be in touch," the man said.

"Grayson."

Tanner folded his arms across his chest and met Frank's gaze. "Scarlett? She's too good for you. And now she knows all about you."

"Rhodes, let's go," his superior said.

"My pleasure. My job here is done."

✧　✧　✧

TANNER WALKED INTO the gym, anger pouring through him in waves. Emotion he had to unleash before he went to see Scarlett. He wished he was just going to bring her lunch and everything was normal but it wasn't. Vic was out of prison and she needed to know about his past and hear it from him.

They strode through the large workout area. Because it was past nine a.m., most people were at work and the gym was on the quieter side. Although he ought to be exhausted, he'd gotten no sleep after the cops left and he and the guys talked late into the night, he was revving for a fight.

"Come on. Let's get some of this aggression out of you," Landon, who'd been silent and let Tanner brood, said as they approached the big black bag in the corner.

Tanner sat while Landon wrapped his hands, protecting his skin and knuckles from the beating he'd otherwise take, then slipped the gloves over his hands.

Landon held the bag while Tanner went off,

punching at the heavy bag, pretending it was Vic's face and body he pummeled, as he worked his hands and unleashed his anger and frustration on the inanimate object. The son of a bitch had changed his life forever, destroyed his dream of showing his bastard father he was better than the man believed.

College? Gone because he'd gone off on another member of the fraternity and gotten himself thrown out in the wake of Levi's death. Levi, full of life and fun, his entire future ahead of him ... dead. Running from the demons in his head, he'd ended up in jail after a bar fight gone bad. Tanner knew he had himself to blame for the wrong turns he'd taken. But Victor was the devil inside him he needed to exorcise.

Hit after hit, sweat poured down his face and onto the floor until he was heaving and finally needed a break. He stopped, leaning down, hands braced on his thighs as he caught his breath.

Landon collapsed onto the bench beside him, also breathing hard from handling the bag while Tanner went off.

The ring of his cell phone sounded and he grabbed it from the bag on the floor. Scarlett's name flashed on the screen.

Stomach twisting, he answered. "Yeah." He was still finding it hard to pull in air.

"Tanner? We need to talk." Her soft voice penetrated the haze around him left over from his workout.

He inhaled deeply. "We do. I'm at the gym. I can shower and meet you somewhere," he said, not wanting an audience at her office for the things he needed to tell her.

"Let's go to my place. Noon?" she asked, sounding both tired and serious.

He hadn't thought to ask how she'd come to the club last night but he assumed she'd heard it on the scanner at her office or the news. "I'll pick up something to eat and meet you there," he said and disconnected the call.

"You okay?" Landon turned his head toward him.

"Fuck no. I've got to tell the one woman who's ever caught my attention that I fucked up my life and got a pass. She, on the other hand, puts guys like me away." He hung his head, pissed at the turn things had taken.

"I think you're being too hard on yourself and not giving her enough credit. But time will tell. In the meantime, let's hit the showers. You can't go anywhere smelling like this."

"Fuck you," he said with a grin. He really didn't know what he'd do without the guys in his life. They were his family. The people he'd live and die for.

Landon chuckled and they headed for the locker room, where he cleaned his body while he hoped

Scarlett accepted his soul.

✧   ✧   ✧

SCARLETT HAD TOSSED and turned all last night, unable to sleep after the adrenaline rush of first the bomb scare, then Frank's warning about Tanner, and the scary guy who'd seemed to threaten her before disappearing into the dark night. She didn't take the man all that seriously. Plenty of sick people wandered the streets of Manhattan, and she doubted his throat-slashing gesture had been aimed at her. Still, she'd double-checked her locks and had a difficult time falling asleep.

She'd spent the morning going over new evidence with Kyle for the trial that was starting next month, but she'd been unable to put what she'd learned about Tanner out of her mind. She needed to hear his story from him. Draw her own conclusions, make her own judgments.

So she'd called him to meet and now she was heading home for the afternoon.

"For someone who's busy at work, I sure as hell have taken a lot of time off lately," Scarlett muttered, packing up files so she could work after Tanner left. But she was keeping up with her caseload and her boss had no reason to complain. He didn't care where she did her prep as long as it got done.

Once arriving at her apartment, she placed her folders on the edge of the table and changed into comfortable clothes, knowing she'd need the time to pull herself together before seeing Tanner. She had a feeling she'd be listening to an emotional explanation that would need her to merge her conscience and her feelings for him. It wouldn't be easy.

When he still hadn't shown up by the time she headed back into her living room, she sat down to work, going through some depositions she'd taken and intended to use for trial.

By the time the doorbell rang, she'd been deep in thought, and the sound startled her. She blew out a deep breath and walked over, opening the door to let Tanner in. "Hi."

She couldn't help but look him over appreciatively, her gaze going from his messily styled hair to the scruff of beard she found so attractive, to the way he filled out his jeans and long-sleeve light blue top, bringing out the color in his eyes.

"Hey." He shoved his hands into his front pockets. "I'm here, ready to talk."

She swallowed hard and nodded. "Good. Come on in."

He stepped in and she shut the door behind him, then led him to the family room. All she could think of was the last time he'd been here and they went straight to the bedroom. No awkwardness between them at all.

Now? Not so much.

✧   ✧   ✧

TANNER FOLLOWED SCARLETT into the main room of her apartment, watching the sway of her sexy hips as she walked. She'd answered the door looking edible in a pair of black leggings and a cropped sweatshirt with the neck cut off and dipping down over one shoulder. He'd wanted nothing more than to pull her into his arms for a kiss, but he felt the distant vibes she was giving off and decided not to. At least not yet.

It was anyone's guess if he'd have that opportunity again after he told her everything. As much as he wanted to be here with Scarlett, he wasn't looking forward to this heart-to-heart. Knowing he had no choice, he braced himself as she settled onto the couch and he took a seat beside her.

"Everything okay after the bomb threat?" she asked.

"Yes … and no."

She narrowed her gaze.

"Look. I saw you with Frank Rhodes, so you obviously know things about me you want answers to." He hadn't meant to sound so defensive but he couldn't control the bite to his words. He curled his hands into fists beside him, then realized and released his grip and forced air into his lungs. He needed to relax and just deal with it.

She nodded. "He mentioned a few things about you and your past, but honestly, I don't put stock into what someone else tells me. I want to hear about you from you."

"What if what Frank told you was true?" Even if the asshole had embellished, Tanner didn't see how the man could make his past sound any worse than it actually had been.

She glanced across the room at the picture of her brother, then clearly forced her gaze back to his. "Why don't you just talk to me and we'll go from there?"

Unable to sit still, he rose and paced the room. "I told you about Levi."

Sadness filled her expression. "Yes."

"Well … even before Levi died, I had issues. Anger issues. I suppose you could say they stemmed from my father, who was a complete asshole. I couldn't react to his verbal abuse the way I really wanted to, so I internalized my feelings. That caused me to act out. You could say despite being a smart guy academically, I was a troublemaker." He smiled ruefully and she laughed.

"I'm sorry about your dad, I think I told you that once before, but that sounds pretty self-aware."

"Therapy."

She raised an eyebrow. "An enlightened man. I'm impressed."

He frowned and said, "Don't be. It was a prerequisite to my partners helping me out of a bind." If he could call a potential prison sentence a bind.

She pulled her bottom lip between her teeth and he wished it was his mouth biting those luscious lips. "I think you need to explain from the beginning," she said.

He blew out a breath, walked to the window, and looked out at the building next door. "After Levi died, the older guys involved were expelled from school and some were arrested, made deals, or went to trial and ended up in jail. But some stayed around town, it was Manhattan after all, and I ran into Vic. He was out on bail. We got into it. I beat him up on campus and got myself thrown out too."

Tanner cleared his throat but he didn't turn around to face her, and she remained silent, as if sensing he needed to gather his thoughts because there was more to tell.

"I spiraled after that." It was as if he was determined to prove his father right, that he wasn't going to make anything of himself. "I was at a bar. I'm not going to make excuses and say that I was defending someone's honor … I was looking for a fight and I got one. I also got myself arrested for assaulting one of the patrons."

"What happened?" Scarlett asked. "Because obviously you wouldn't be able to own a club or be given a liquor license if you had a felony on your record."

He ignored the edge of judgment in her tone. "Jason reached out to his cousin Gabriel Dare. Gabe has friends in high places. Essentially he got me an executive pardon. And I promised my friends, men I consider brothers, that I'd get help in order to control my anger. I did community service to put my head in the right space, I saw a therapist who taught me how to channel my anger – boxing, breathing exercises, things like that. And I promised them they'd never have an issue with me again."

"It was that easy? A promise, some therapy, and you didn't pay for your crime?"

He spun around, pissed at her callously thrown out words. "I paid every damn day. I'm still paying. But before you judge me, know this. I'm betting the difference between me and the guys who killed your brother is that I have *remorse*."

Awareness and regret flashed in her eyes. She'd lashed out at him because of her own pain. Which meant this was his chance to get through to her. To let her see the real man inside him.

He strode up to her and met her gaze. "I regret beating the shit out of Vic…" If only because it hurt the guys in the end too. "And I regret going after the asshole in the bar. I hate this angry part of me that I work to keep under control. But other than the man at the bar who had the misfortune to piss me off at the lowest point of my life, the only people I've ever touched are those who hurt people I care about. Me, my sister, the men I consider brothers." He held up a hand before she could misinterpret his words. "That's not an excuse. It's wrong. And I work every day to make it right."

She exhaled a long breath. "I see."

"Do you? Or do you look at me and see someone who's no better than the guys who walked on a technicality after your brother died? Do you judge me for my past?"

Time ticked by as he waited for her to answer. Time that felt like an eternity but was only a few seconds. Time that let him stare at her pale but beautiful features and realize he was more addicted to this woman than he'd wanted to admit.

"I—" She paused, then drew a deep breath. "I can't say I'm happy with what you told me. And accepting it makes me feel like a hypocrite after promising my brother, at his gravesite, I'd put criminals behind bars and make people pay for their crimes. How you acted, how you worked the system, despite it being legal, goes against everything I believe in."

He stiffened his shoulders, prepared for her to throw him out.

She reached out and cupped his face in her hand. "But I've also gotten to know you. The man standing in front of me now, and I know you're a decent man." She shook her head. "I have to work through this in my head. But I can't just walk away from you either."

"Thank fuck." He stepped forward and pulled her into his arms.

When she tipped her head, he took the hint and covered her mouth with his. He kissed her with all the relief he felt and the desire that never failed to consume him when she was around. He didn't kid himself that they'd turned a corner. He knew he had more to prove. But she hadn't gone running. And that was enough for now.

✧　✧　✧

SCARLETT'S HEAD WAS spinning and not because of that kiss, but she had to admit she liked being in Tanner's arms. Although she'd already had an inkling of his history from Frank, getting confirmation from him that he'd been arrested for assault and gotten off easily hurt. Then again so did hearing about the fact that he'd been so bullied by his own father as a child, he'd channeled his aggression internally until he'd acted out. No parent should treat a child that way.

A nightclub owner with a shady past, he was the antithesis of the goals she'd set out for her life. Yet he was everything she wanted. And Scarlett didn't deal well with contradictions, something she sensed Tanner understood because after that kiss, he'd taken a step back. And was studying her like he expected her to change her mind at any moment.

"I need you to do me a favor," Tanner said.

That was a surprising request. "Okay. What is it?"

"Can you find out how someone got out of prison earlier than they should have?"

She nodded. "Who?"

"Victor Clark."

She blinked in shock. "You mean the same Victor who killed Levi?"

He groaned. "Yeah. I saw him outside last night after the bomb threat evacuation."

She cocked her head to the side. "How'd you react?"

A reluctant frown pulled at his sexy lips. "Instinct took over. I started to go after him." He paused. "But Landon put a hand on my shoulder. His touch brought me back to the present. The truth is the guys dragged me out of the alley and away from temptation."

She knew how difficult it must be for him to admit the truth to her when he was trying to convince her he'd changed.

"At least you're honest." He could have said it had been no problem seeing Victor again.

"I don't see the point in lying to you. You'd figure out who I really am soon enough." Despite the seriousness of their conversation, he winked and her girlie parts stood up and took notice.

How was she supposed to think with her brain when her body just wanted to jump him where he stood?

"So you'll find out about Victor?" He brought them back to the point at hand.

She nodded. "I'll give you a call as soon as I find out something."

"Thank you." He started for the door.

His sudden departure took her off guard. "Why are you leaving?"

"I'm going to give you time to work through things in that pretty head of yours. You know where to find me." He walked out, shutting the door behind him.

Alone, she returned to the living room and settled on the couch, wondering why life threw the one man in her path who challenged her on every level. The one man she couldn't resist.

Chapter Seven

"**G**OOD MORNING!" LEIGH popped her head into Scarlett's office. "I hear someone's going to be doing actual witness questioning in court next month!" She slid into the chair she always chose and crossed her legs in front of her. "Go you."

Scarlett grinned. "Kyle told me this morning during our team meeting."

"I told you you're proving yourself. That's a huge case for him to loosen the reins on."

"I'm happy." Scarlett folded her hands on her desk and glanced at her friend. "So? How's things?"

"Same old. How's your mom?"

Scarlett scrunched up her nose. "Not great. My dad's now able to sign off on her getting ECT since she's a threat to herself ... but he's scared to do it. He's afraid she'll blame him and be angry. Not that she's had any real emotion in so long. But I understand how tough a decision it is for him. I don't blame him for struggling."

She'd visited her mother once a week since she'd

been put in the home, but nothing had changed. No acknowledgment of her presence, nothing. The sad truth was that Scarlett had long since given up hope of having her mom in her life as a real presence. She'd done enough reading that she wasn't even convinced that ECT would bring her back after all this time.

"Okay so on to happier things, how's your hot guy?" Leigh changed the subject.

"How's *your* hot guy?" Scarlett threw back at her friend.

Leigh held up her hands and laughed. "Fine. I'll go first. Cliff is awesome. He texts during the day, he isn't pulling away or acting like a commitment-phobe ... so far really good!" She leaned in closer. "I answered you, so now you can't avoid my question. How's your club owner?"

"He's ... complicated, Leigh. He's got what amounts to an expunged record for assault and yet he's a good guy. I can sense that in him." And she'd been around enough criminals to know the difference.

"Honey, relationships are complicated. And it's a known fact that opposites attract. So you like a bad boy. This isn't a terrible thing."

"Maybe, maybe not." She'd tossed and turned last night, unable to reconcile his past and the promise she'd made crying over her brother's grave. "I need to think about how I really feel."

"Don't think too long. A guy who looks like him won't be on the market for long," Leigh said as she twirled a strand of her brown hair around her finger. "Know what I mean?"

Scarlett ignored that comment. "Listen, I need to make a call," she said as she picked up the phone on her desk.

For Tanner.

"Sure. I have work to do. Catch you later!" Leigh stood and left the room.

Scarlett opened her computer and pulled up Victor Clark's mug shot. His face filled the screen and she opened her mouth in shock. "That's the guy who threatened me at the club."

She immediately grabbed her cell, the desire to tell Tanner overwhelming, but she paused, putting the phone down and forcing herself to think. Tanner had a history with Victor, one that pushed his buttons and caused him to act out. Did she really want to tell Tanner the man he despised had threatened her? He'd beaten up Victor once before.

She glanced at the screen and shivered, finding it difficult to convince herself it was a coincidence that he'd been hanging around the club the night of the bomb scare, that he'd threatened her, and didn't know she was connected to Tanner.

Based on her knowledge of cops, even if she mentioned the situation to friends on the force, they'd tell her there was nothing they could do with what amounted to a threatening gesture. Which meant she was on her own. Unless she told Tanner. He deserved to know. And she couldn't deny this would be a test of how well he handled his temper these days.

With shaking hands, she found and touched his number.

"Scarlett?" He answered immediately.

"Can you come to my office? Now?" she asked, closing out of the page because she did not want to look into those cold eyes another second longer.

"I'll be right over."

While she waited, she made use of the time it would take him to show up. Picking up the phone, she made a few calls. It wasn't difficult for her to find out in which prison Victor had been incarcerated. From there, another couple of leads and she'd discovered how and why he'd been tagged for early release, giving her the answers Tanner wanted.

"Mail call!" Marty, the intern pushed a cart as he knocked and stepped into Scarlett's office. "This came for you, Ms. Davis." He handed her a plain manila envelope addressed to Scarlett Davis, Esquire.

"Thanks, Marty." She accepted the flat packet and he walked out, heading for his next office stop.

She held the envelope and glanced at both sides.

"That's odd. No return address. Hmm." Slicing it open, she pulled out a white sheet of paper with red writing.

You're dead.

No signature.

Her stomach turned over at the sight, her mind immediately going to Vic and his threatening gesture. She dropped the letter and called for forensics to come pick it up, though she knew, like most evidence delivered here, there wouldn't be fingerprints or anything to find.

All she could do now was wait for Tanner.

TANNER HADN'T EXPECTED to hear from Scarlett any time soon. He assumed she'd need time to decide how she felt about his past, and he'd had every intention of giving her the space she deserved. So when his phone rang and she asked to see him, to say he'd been shocked was an understatement. If she merely had discovered information on Victor, she could have just told him over the phone. His gut screamed something deeper was at play.

He crossed town and arrived at her office as fast as he could get there, opting for the subway to take him the fastest way, cutting out traffic.

Michelle, a full-figured woman at the front desk

who knew him by now, waved him on by. Scarlett's office door was closed, so he knocked and waited for her to tell him to come in.

At the sound of her voice, he pushed open the door and stepped inside, shutting it behind him when he realized they were alone.

"Hey. Is everything okay?" he asked, out of breath from the way he'd rushed to get here.

She toyed with the pen on her desk, biting into her bottom lip as she met his gaze. Clearly something was very wrong.

"Talk to me," he said, walking over and sitting on the edge of her desk, close enough to be affected by her peach scent.

"Fine. First things first." She glanced at a paper on her desk with her handwriting on it. "I made the call you asked and I know how Victor acquired early release. Simple answer to that question. He snitched on his cellmate to the feds. Gave them information they needed to close a huge drug case, and in exchange, he walked early."

"Son of a bitch." His hands immediately curled but he caught the movement before he formed fists. Instead he forced air into his lungs, aware of her watching him warily. "Okay, at least I have my answer."

"There's more."

"Okay…" He braced himself and waited.

"Something happened the other night and I didn't mention it before because I brushed it off. I thought … well, it's Manhattan. I figured it was just a crazy person. And–"

He grabbed her hands, which she was wringing in front of her as she spoke, clearly upset. "Scarlett? You can tell me anything."

She visibly swallowed hard. "Okay, well, when I was outside the club the night of the bomb scare, a guy I'd never seen before looked at me. He smiled in this really creepy way and then he took his finger and sliced it across his neck. Like this."

She repeated the gesture and Tanner's blood ran cold. He didn't like the idea of anyone threatening her, especially outside of his club. "You should have told me."

She rolled her shoulders. "You and your partners had already disappeared. You'd probably gone inside. I yelled for Frank, the cop, but when I pointed to show him the man, he wasn't there."

Worry and concern wrapped icy tentacles around him. "What aren't you saying?"

Her wide eyes met his. "When I pulled up Victor's mug shot, I recognized him. *He* was the guy who threatened me."

"That bastard is using you to get to me." Anger

and pain lanced through him.

She nodded. "I had that thought myself although I'd prefer if it was a coincidence."

He shook his head. "There are no coincidences where Victor is concerned." Ignoring the rush of blood to his head that signaled the anger that always accompanied thoughts of Vic, first and foremost, he focused on Scarlett. "If he's targeting you, it's because of me."

She looked at him, utterly calm. "I've been the subject of threats before. It's all in a day's work in this job." She even smiled to reassure him.

It didn't work. "You don't know this man. I do."

"Okay, well … I received a threat today."

His gaze whipped to hers. "What?"

She opened her phone and showed him a photo. "I took this before I had forensics take it to examine. And before you get upset and jump to conclusions, it could be related to the mob case I'm working on."

He narrowed his gaze. "You don't believe that any more than I do. It's Vic. Showing me he can get to you." Tanner pulled out his phone and began to text.

"What are you doing?" she asked.

"Calling a meeting. I want to talk to Jason and Landon. Fill them in." It was his fault Scarlett was in the middle of this.

"Tanner, I also spoke to one of the cops who

works with us. They're aware, not that there's anything they can do with nonspecific threats."

He heard the calming tone in her voice, but it wasn't working to soothe him. This was all Vic and it was his fault she was in his sights.

"Okay, well, if that's all, I have a lot of work to get through today." She patted the top of a pile of case files with a fake smile on her face.

He shook his head. "I want you in the meeting." He was already working up a plan on how to protect her. One she wasn't going to like and he wanted backup when he presented it to her. Landon would help. Jason would be the key because he'd been in a similar situation with Faith and taken comparable action.

Hmm. Maybe he should have Faith there too. He continued to text the guys, making his wishes clear.

"Tanner, come on. There's no reason for me to be in on a meeting about Vic. He doesn't know who I am. He…"

"Might have been following me all the times I brought you lunch. Or when we went out. How else would he know you to single you out the other night?"

She groaned. "After work then, okay?" This time she *pointed* to the pile of work, exasperation in her features.

She wasn't taking this as seriously as he was, but

that was because she didn't know what Victor Clark was capable of. Tanner did. And after over a decade in prison? Yeah. No way would Tanner blow off the man's threat. It was all he could do to remain calm. Not to lose his mind and scare her away.

He glanced at his phone. Both Jason and Landon would be at the club this evening and Jason said he'd bring Faith. "I'll pick you up after work," Tanner told Scarlett. "Name the time."

"Seven? I really have a lot to get done. I can meet you at the club—"

He shook his head. "I'll be here."

He confirmed the time with his partners and tried not to focus on the fact that Scarlett was in danger because of him. But he couldn't shake off the feeling of responsibility he felt toward her. Partly because Vic was involved and more because his heart was.

SCARLETT WALKED INTO Club TEN29, and with Tanner's hand on her back, he led her to the elevator and up to the office, where his partners waited. She hated to admit the pull she felt toward him, how much she liked the heat of his palm against her shirt, the possessive way he touched her. As if telling everyone around him to back off. She was taken.

Although the club wasn't that busy, it being early

in the week, she noted a big security guard was present, arms folded across his chest. Apparently the guys were taking no chances, because she didn't remember him being so visible the last time she was here.

This was the first time she would be meeting Tanner's partners and close friends, and it was under a stressful situation. Although she didn't know what he planned, the fact that he wanted her present for the conversation meant it involved her in some way beyond the obvious.

They entered the doorway and the low murmur of conversation stopped, all eyes focused on her. She looked over the two men she'd seen on the website and then saw Faith, Jason's wife, sitting close to her husband.

"Faith! What are you doing here?" Scarlett asked.

The other woman was dressed similarly to the day they'd met, in a pair of jeans and a Sweet Treats tee shirt. Obviously, she too had come straight from work.

Faith glanced at Jason, then rose from her seat. "You'll see soon enough." She glared at the men in the room.

"Scarlett, I'd like you to meet my partners and best friends, Jason Dare, Faith's husband, and Landon Bennett. You already know Faith," Tanner said.

Landon walked over and took her hand. "Nice to meet you."

"I've heard a lot about you," Jason said with a grin, earning himself a nudge from his wife. "All of it good," he rushed to add.

"Thank you." Scarlett glanced at Tanner for guidance on this meeting.

"Here. Let's sit." He gestured to the couch and led her to the sofa, where he settled in beside her. "Thanks for being here, everyone. I've had the afternoon to fill them in on the situation and the fact that Vic knows who you are and has targeted you."

She raised her hands and dropped them to her lap. "We don't know that," she reminded him. And the rest of them, for that matter.

"However, we do know that Vic has it in for our club," Landon said, leaning against his desk, a powerful presence in his black jacket, white dress shirt, and black slacks. Nightclub ready, she mused.

"We've had issues with Daniel Sutherland, another club owner, targeting us for petty vandalism, but there is the fact that if Vic is going to go after anyone, it's going to be Tanner." Jason spoke.

"Because he beat him up on campus years ago?" Scarlett asked.

"No, because I'm the weak link," Tanner muttered.

She hated his self-deprecation and reached out to squeeze his hand in silent support before letting go.

He continued to scowl as he spoke. "And since

I'm the one whose buttons Vic can push hard enough to make me go after him."

His words surprised her. Yes, he knew himself, but he'd also gone to great lengths to convince her he'd learned to manage his temper. Was he changing his mind?

"I wouldn't have phrased it like that," Jason said with a scowl. "But if he wants to get to any of us, I agree he'll choose you."

"Because at the very least he believes I'll be the one to lose my shit and end up behind bars." Tanner shook his head. "Retribution at its finest. And that puts you at risk," he said, once again taking Scarlett's hand in his larger one.

She cleared her throat, ignoring the warmth of his touch. "As I told you, I've dealt with threats before in my line of work. I can handle myself."

"But you've never dealt with Victor Clark. And since you're in trouble because of me, I'm going to be the one to protect you." He rose to his feet, a large, looming, *sexy* presence.

She raised an eyebrow at the same time Jason, who sat across the room, Faith now beside him, snickered under his breath.

Faith slapped his arm. "Cut that out."

"What's so funny?" Scarlett asked.

Faith sighed. "He's just listening to Tanner butter

you up so he can step in and take care of you. Sort of like Jason did for me."

Scarlett thought about Faith's situation with her brother, recalled her explanation of what had happened. "You already mentioned you had some problems and Jason moved you in with him... Oh, no," she said, realizing exactly what this meeting was about. "That is not happening in this case."

"Here's the situation and correct me if I'm wrong." Tanner paced, something she was coming to learn he did when he was upset. "Victor is targeting our club. It's looking like he's teamed up with Sutherland to bash cars, graffiti walls, and even gone so far as a bomb threat ... but we can't prove it was him. With me so far?"

She inclined her head. "Yes."

He stopped his pacing directly in front of her. "You saw Victor outside the club, he looked right at you and..." Tanner duplicated the neck gesture, never breaking eye contact. "Yes?"

She squirmed in her seat. "Yes."

Across from her, the guys and Faith were silent. She didn't take that as a good sign that they were on her side.

"And today you received a threatening note in what looked like blood." Tanner's eyes turned darker.

She shivered. She'd tried not to think about *that*

part of the note. But he was right. "Again, correct. But for some reason you think this means I need to *move in with you*?"

"I think you need protection. Will your cop friends help you?" He cocked his head to the side. "Or will they continue to tell you there's nothing they can do without proof of who's targeting you?"

She narrowed her gaze, hating that he was right. She was an independent woman who'd been taking care of herself for longer than most people. She held a difficult job that often came with risks. And she'd never been afraid. Until now.

Tanner lowered himself into the seat beside her, moving in closer, bracketing her with his body heat. "I'm going to repeat, you don't know who you're dealing with. We do. I already blame myself for not protecting Levi. I couldn't handle it if anything happened to you because of me."

She might have been able to fight the first part of his statement. Every defendant she dealt with was dangerous given the right circumstances. But she couldn't handle the second part of his pronouncement. The emotional part. The self-recrimination and blame he felt were something she understood. She felt them about her brother. The inability to protect the person she loved.

But Tanner didn't love her. They weren't even

close to being a couple. So why did he feel so protective of her? And why did she feel the same way about him and want to do as he asked so he didn't punish himself for things that weren't his fault?

But to move in with him? She glanced at Faith. "How did you do it? How did you just—"

"Move in with a man I didn't know?" Faith grinned. "Something about him was trustworthy. And he didn't give me a choice." She looked at Jason like he was everything she needed in her life.

And a part of Scarlett she hadn't known existed twisted with jealousy. Not over Jason but over the fact that Faith had someone in her life who meant so much to her … and that she reciprocated those feelings.

Scarlett turned to Tanner and her stomach twisted with an emotion she was too afraid to dissect. "You really think Victor is after me?"

"I know I don't trust him not to hurt you to get to me. Or to us." Tanner's gaze encompassed his partners. "I have no idea what's going on in that sadistic brain of his."

"I'm going back to watching Faith twenty-four seven," Jason said. "If that makes you feel any better."

Faith grinned when she looked at Jason. "I like you watching my body twenty-four seven."

He slid a hand up the back of her shirt. "It's certainly not a hardship, sweetness."

"Oh, Jesus." Landon rolled his eyes.

Chuckling, Tanner looked at Scarlett. "So what's it going to be? I have a house in Queens."

She blinked in surprise. "A house?"

"Yeah. He didn't want to be confined in an apartment," Landon said before Tanner could explain.

"Fuck," Tanner muttered. "I spent some time behind bars. It was enough for me. I wanted space. So sue me."

Her heart squeezed inside her chest. Moving in with him seemed extreme … and yet when she thought about Victor's cold eyes, maybe not. From the moment Tanner had been honest with her about his past, she hadn't had a chance to truly process her feelings for him. Instead she'd had one hit after another, from Victor being the one who threatened her to the menacing note sent to her office to moving in with him now.

Scarlett prided herself on being rational, and given that fact, she realized Tanner was a good man who'd overcome his past. And that meant he deserved a second chance. And he obviously wanted to take care of her now.

"I have to be at the office on time every morning." It was her way of letting him know she was agreeing to his demand.

He released a relieved breath. "You will be," he

promised.

"And how long will this be for?" She curled her hand around her purse.

The men glanced at each other.

"Until we find proof against Vic and get him behind bars. We have a private investigator working on it." Tanner met her gaze, gratitude filling his expression.

He really was worried about her, she realized, her heart softening toward him even more. That same heart told her that when it came to this man, she was in a lot of trouble.

Chapter Eight

AFTER THE MEETING, Tanner took Scarlett in his Range Rover to her apartment to pack her things. Rain came down heavily as he drove, requiring his concentration. She was silent, so he left her to her thoughts, knowing he'd sprung the move on her and she was coming, if not under duress, then somewhat hesitantly.

He approached the street, taking in the neighborhood as he always did, with a sense of pleasure and pride. He had always wanted a place of his own. A home, not an apartment that felt temporary. Once he and the guys opened the club and the business took off, he felt comfortable investing in a piece of property. Unlike his friends, who had apartments in Manhattan, he wanted to look outside and see green grass. Trees.

And thanks to the apartment above the club, he'd never had to bring a woman home to intrude on his solitude and private space. Which had worked for him until he'd laid eyes on Scarlett. To his shock and surprise, he'd been wanting to show her his house. To have her in his home, so her scent lingered and he could envision her there even when she wasn't around.

As he pulled up to the house, he realized he cared what she thought of this place he loved. It was a classic Tudor-style home on one third of an acre in Forest Hills Gardens, and he took satisfaction in the manicured gardens he paid a fortune to keep up.

"This is it." As he approached the house, Scarlett pushed herself upright in her seat, focusing on the Tudor in front of her.

"It's gorgeous," she said as he turned into the long driveway. "I have to admit I never pictured you in a neighborhood."

Hand on the steering wheel, he turned his head and met her gaze. "I hope I continue to surprise you in all the best ways," he said with a wink.

She blew out a breath. "If all but demanding I move in with you is your idea of a good surprise, I can't imagine what's next."

He chuckled under his breath. "I merely encouraged you."

"By using emotional blackmail."

I already blame myself for not protecting Levi. I couldn't handle it if anything happened to you because of me.

He didn't bother denying it. Instead he shrugged. "Every word was true. And it worked." This way he knew she was safe under his roof and with him when she wasn't at work.

He pulled into the garage and put the SUV in park. "Come on. I'll give you the grand tour."

"Looking forward to it." She hopped out of her side, and he grabbed her suitcase and carried it into the house, leaving it by the main-floor stairway.

He showed her around the bottom floor. An arched doorway led to a main entry with the original hardwood floors. "This is the living room." He gestured to a large room that opened to a banquet-sized dining room. "Dining room. Which obviously never gets used..." He grinned and cast a glance her way.

Her eyes were wide. "I love the warmth of the house and the wood accents. And the neutral colors with pops of burgundy? It's beautiful."

"Decorator," he admitted as they stepped into a breakfast room and beyond was the French-style kitchen. "It was recently renovated when I bought it, so I left this room alone."

"Good call." She smiled. "I am not a cook but someone who is would love to work in there."

"Takeout tastes just as good as homemade food in my book," he assured her. He wasn't throwing her out of his life because she didn't prepare meals. So far she seemed to have forgiven his past, though they hadn't had a deep conversation about it yet either. His status was still tenuous.

As they walked through the rest of the downstairs, a library he'd turned into a man-cave and the big den with a huge-screen television, her compliments continued, which pleased him. He didn't understand the warmth in his chest or why he cared. He'd gone all his life without approval from his father, the people who should have given it unconditionally, but what this woman thought meant something to him.

"The master is on the top floor and there are three rooms on the second level." He turned by her suitcase and she stopped short, very little space between them. "The question is do you want to sleep alone? Or with me?"

Her luscious lips parted in surprise.

"Are you still unsure about me?" He leaned against the bannister, eyes focused on her. And if his desire was evident by the tenting in his pants and the pounding of his heart, hers was visible in the way she looked at him, her darkened irises and intent expression.

"No. I'm not unsure."

At her words, relief spread through him.

"Everyone has a past and I can see that you've overcome yours." Her gaze warmed along with her words and he moved in closer.

"Do you trust me enough to give us a try?" When

she didn't answer immediately, he swept a finger over her parted lips. "You have to admit this takes care of your 'no time for anything but work' problem. We'll be together before and after hours."

"Don't *you* have work?" She raised an eyebrow. "Work that involves you spending evenings at the club?"

"I would if something else didn't take priority. Like your safety. I have partners who are more than willing to step in. I did it for Jason when he needed to be with Faith."

She darted her tongue out and licked his finger, his cock perking up at the not-so-innocent gesture. "You're making it very difficult to say no to you."

"Only because I'm so tempting," he said with a grin. "And because our first couple of times were so hot you're dying for a repeat performance."

She smiled, clearly having relaxed around him. "Someone's getting cocky."

"Because someone's not saying no."

She stepped forward and laced her arms around his neck, pulling him close until his erection rubbed against her. "That's because you're a hard man to turn down, Mr. Grayson."

He grinned and lifted her into his arms.

"Tanner! What are you doing?" she squealed holding on to his neck.

"Settling you in my room," he said as he started up the stairs. "I'll come back for your bag." Right now he wanted to focus on getting her into his bed.

Once in his room, he deposited her on the mattress with a bounce and she grinned. Climbing to her knees, she pushed herself to the edge of the bed and grabbed his jeans, popping them open and unzipping his fly.

He stilled as she proceeded to wriggle his pants down over his hips and thighs, taking his boxer briefs along with them, freeing his cock. He was so fucking hard, pre-come seeped from the head.

"Come lie down," she said, gripping him in her fist and pumping her hand up and down, causing him to groan.

But she scooted backwards and he did as she said, stretching himself out on the bed. "You're going to kill me before we get started."

"You'll enjoy it though." She bent her head and licked his shaft and an electric current seemed to run through him as his body jerked at her wet touch. Then she opened her mouth and took him inside.

He slid his hands into her hair, doing his best to watch her sexy lips moving over his dick. He wrapped the long strands around his hand and tugged as she sucked him deep into her mouth. The suction felt so good his eyes nearly rolled back in his head, and he closed them, giving himself over to her sexy ministrations. But he couldn't stop his hips from bucking, pushing himself deeper into her mouth with every pass.

Heaven couldn't come close to what he was experiencing now. As one of her hands ran up and down his cock, her mouth followed. His dick was bathed in warm, wet heat and pulsing waves of desire washed over him. This might as well have been the first blow job he'd ever had the way his body was reacting so quickly. For damn sure it was the best, and he knew it was because it was Scarlett's lips sucking him deep. Nothing had ever felt as good.

He was lost in sensation, aware of only the pulsing in his dick that told him he was seconds away from coming. His balls drew up and his spine tingled, both warning signs. This time he tugged at her hair for a different reason, to warn her. But instead of releasing him, she hollowed her cheeks and sucked him harder and faster until his climax hit with unreal force as pleasure rocked him to his core. And she kept up with him, swallowing as his orgasm peaked and finally ended, leaving him wrecked in the best possible way.

He released his tight hold on her hair and ran his fingers through the strands as she lifted her head and met his gaze, a satisfied smile on her wet, swollen lips.

"C'mere," he said in a gruff voice.

She scooted up into the crook of his arm and he pulled her up and kissed her, tasting himself as he thrust his tongue into her eager mouth. Gratitude felt stupid but that's what he was. Grateful for what she'd given him. She'd showed him that she accepted him, all of him, who he'd been and who he was now.

He pulled back, meeting her gaze. "That was fucking amazing."

"It was, wasn't it?" She grinned.

"Someone's pleased with herself."

She laughed, then pushed herself up to a sitting position and began to strip out of her clothes. She lifted her camisole off and tossed it to the floor. Her lacy bra followed.

And though she reached for the button on the back of her skirt, he sidetracked her, sitting up and capturing one nipple between his teeth.

"Aaah." She moaned as he tugged, then pulled that same tight bud into his mouth and licked, nibbled, and lapped at her until her hips were making unwitting circular motions, desire getting the best of her.

He gripped her waist, holding her still as he switched to the other side and gave it equal sensual treatment. As he devoured her breasts, he reached around and unzipped her skirt, which pooled around her knees. He released her nipple with a pop, then helped her out of the rest of her clothes, lay down on the bed, looked at her beautifully naked body.

"Straddle me," he said, eager to get a taste of her. Frankly he wanted to fuck her, but even he needed a few minutes to catch his breath.

She placed her legs on either side of his waist and he chuckled. "Not what I meant, sweetheart," he said and crooked his finger toward her.

Eyes opened wide, she shimmied upward, sliding forward as he continued to coax her farther until she was positioned where he wanted her, over his mouth. Grasping her thighs, he urged her to lower herself and she did, so he could swipe his tongue over her sex. Her taste turned him on and he felt the tingling in his cock. Yeah, he'd be ready in no time. Meanwhile, he was going to take her on a ride.

He slid his tongue over her again and she moaned and gave in, dropping her body lower so he could devour her. And he did. As he licked, sucked, and slid his tongue over and around, she rocked herself against him, grinding her sweet pussy against his mouth. She must have been primed and ready because it didn't take long before he recognized the telltale signs she was close.

Her body trembled, a low, throaty groan echoed around him, and she shook as he stiffened his tongue and thrust inside her. She cried out, her body tightened, and her inner muscles contracted around him as she came, her soft cries of pleasure combined with calling his name.

He waited until she'd ridden out her climax, then lifted her up and off him and rolled her to her back, coming over her, his cock stiff and aching. Unable to wait another second, he slid into her, her wetness making it a smooth glide as he entered her completely.

The second he was inside her, he knew. From the intimacy of bare skin to bare skin to the incredible way she felt around him... "Fuck. Condom." He immediately pulled out, cursing himself. He never screwed around without one.

Not that anything he felt for Scarlett was remotely like the cold, distant sex he'd grown used to before her.

"Come back. I'm on the pill," she said, moaning at the loss.

He met her gaze and something warm and wonderful passed between them. "I'm clean. I've been tested since the last time I... Well, I just know I'm safe. But are you sure?" Because he knew from that one pass inside her, sex without a barrier between them meant *more*.

She threaded her fingers through his hair and nodded. "I'm sure."

He pushed back into her, taking his time. Now that he was aware, he wanted to savor every second of this first time. And it really did feel different. Her inner walls clasped him tight and he groaned.

"Fuck, Scarlett, you feel like heaven." He raised his hips and pulled out before gliding home again.

Her eyes glazed over. "Do that again," she said in a sexy, husky voice.

Bracing his hands beside her, he slid out and in, her heady moan not only encouraging him to keep up the motion but arousing him to the point of desperation. He began to thrust into her, over and over, a constant arch of his back and slam of his hips.

She raised her legs and hooked them around his back, the position enabling him to take her harder and deeper with each pass. She was with him every step of the way, her body in sync with his, her slick wetness coating his cock.

He'd never felt emotion during sex. Hell, he didn't think he'd ever *felt* anything like this before in his life. This woman had a vise-like grip on his heart as strong as the one she currently had on his dick. Which meant she had the power to break him, he thought.

Before he could panic over that, she began to shake around him, her climax sudden and clearly huge. He let her ride out the waves before giving in to his own, the rush of feeling that poured through him in that moment overwhelming.

✧　✧　✧

THE NEXT MORNING, Scarlett and Tanner showered separately, agreeing that if they walked into the room together, she'd never get to work on time. Because she'd already been up all night having the best sex of her life.

It had been more than just sex, she thought, as she stepped into the steaming shower and began to wash, using his masculine-smelling soap. She mentally tacked a trip to the store to buy her own brand of products onto her to-do list because she couldn't go around smelling like Tanner. As much as she liked being wrapped in his familiar, musky scent.

Body washed, she turned to her hair, tipping her head beneath the spray. The bathroom was gorgeous with granite and stone on the floor, walls, and counter-tops. As someone who had a postage-stamp-sized bathroom in Manhattan, she could get used to the kind of luxury the entire setup provided.

Which was part of the panic that rushed through her veins after the amazing night they'd shared. The axis on which she operated had shifted and it scared her. From the time Hank had been killed, she'd been solely focused on her goal of getting through school so she could graduate college, then law school and get to work putting criminals behind bars. Her satisfaction came from a job well done and done right, not from her personal life. Hell, she'd never had much of one and she'd never felt lacking.

Maybe because she hadn't come from a functional family unit, she hadn't ever been a girl who dreamed of marriage, children, and a happily ever after. Not when her own mother sat staring out a window all day and her father worked so hard he barely noticed ... until Scarlett had moved out and he'd had to hire a neighbor to look after his wife.

She blinked into the steamy room and conditioned and rinsed her hair, wondering why she was thinking about all these things now. The answer came easily. Because of how Tanner made her feel. Beyond the mind-altering, epic sex they'd had was an emotional connection she'd never shared with anyone before.

On top of that, he made her feel cared for. Settled. Not alone. All things she'd never had in her life, and the tantalizing taste of it now scared her. What if she gave in to the emotions threatening to overwhelm her and this relationship didn't work out? Or what if she let down her walls only to find herself alone again?

Until Tanner, she hadn't realized she had those walls. Being with him opened up a scary world of feeling and emotion she didn't know how to handle. She swallowed hard. Work. She needed to concentrate on work because that was the one thing she knew she could count on. The one thing in her life that made sense and she understood. The rest she'd take as it came and hope for the best.

She stepped out of the bathroom wrapped in fluffy towels, one on her head and the other wrapped around her body, to find Tanner on his cell phone. He'd already dressed and was wearing a pair of jeans that molded to his fine ass and a black long-sleeve shirt, making a drool-worthy package from behind.

He must have sensed her presence, because he turned, his eyes darkening as they took her in. "My sister," he mouthed, pointing to the phone.

She nodded. Clasping the towel in her hand, she went to pick out her clothes for the day, pulling another variation of her usual pair of slacks and a camisole from the suitcase Tanner had brought upstairs late last night.

She hadn't taken the time to unpack because she'd been exhausted. They had, however, fit dinner into their evening. He'd ordered in baked ziti and pizza from a restaurant nearby that delivered.

"Dinner tonight?" she heard him say into the phone.

"Go." This time she mouthed to him.

"I can't tonight," he said instead.

Scarlett felt guilty keeping him from his family. Worse when she heard what he said next.

"I know it's been awhile but things here are"—he glanced at Scarlett and grinned—"complicated."

She rolled her eyes. "Go," she mouthed again. "I'll stay here." She gestured to where she was standing.

He shook his head, his expression stern. "Fine," he said into the phone. "I'll be there but I'm bringing a guest."

Scarlett waved her hands, trying to let him know that she didn't need to go with him to his sister's. That he could leave her here and she'd be perfectly safe. He'd set an alarm last night and she knew she'd be fine alone in the house.

Instead of agreeing, he treated her to a scowl before turning back to his conversation. "Yes. Six is fine. We'll be there."

Scarlett sighed in acceptance. Clearly he was calling the shots. Six was early for her to be somewhere even on a Friday night, but since this was his family, she wasn't going to make him feel bad by complaining she had to work.

He disconnected the call and met her gaze. "I'm sorry. I haven't seen my sister in a while and she pulled the guilt card."

She smiled at his brotherly reaction. "That's okay. But I really could stay here. You could set the alarm and I'd be fine."

He exhaled hard. "That's probably true ... but I

want you to meet her."

She blinked in surprise. "You do? Why?" she blurted out, feeling stupid as soon as the word passed her lips.

A grin on his handsome face, he stepped forward and tipped her chin up with his hand. "Because when a guy likes a girl and he feels like it could get serious, he wants her to meet his family. And other than the guys, Alyssa is the only family I have." Something painful flashed in his expression, distracting her from the nerve-inducing comments about them becoming serious.

"What is your relationship with your parents like these days?" He'd mentioned the fact that his mom was great to him growing up but nothing about her since.

A muscle ticked in his tight jaw. "Ever since she followed my dad's lead in not supporting Alyssa or being there for her when she got pregnant, I wanted them both out of my life, but I was still at home. I had no choices. But even then, I knew that's not what a parent does to their kids."

"I agree," Scarlett said softly, feeling sorry for him and his sister.

He'd begun his pacing, and she held back a grin because she'd come to know him well enough by now to expect it. Tough conversation? The pacing began.

"I already had a shitty relationship with my father. After the guys bailed me out of jail, he had his say, believe me. What a waste of time and space I was. How useless."

His hands curled into tight fists, his knuckles turning white under the strain. Then, as if a light of awareness went on, he blew out a slow breath and released the tension, opening his hands and shaking them out. She narrowed her gaze. He clearly did work at getting ahold of his anger.

He paused in front of her. "I wanted nothing to do with him from that point on. I spoke to my mother once, after we opened the club and things were going well. I asked if she wanted help leaving him. She said no, he was her husband. At which point I figure she made her choice. So I made mine. I cut them out completely."

She touched his cheek, calling his attention to her. "It's their loss. Do you understand me? You're a good man, Tanner. Worth a lot and worth knowing."

Gratitude flashed in his expression, but instead of answering, he leaned over and brushed his lips over hers by way of thanks.

She tilted her head back, expecting him to deepen the kiss when she felt a playful slap on her ass instead. "Hey!"

"Who's the one who said she can't be late for

work?" he asked, winking at her.

Clearly serious conversation was over.

An hour later, Scarlett found herself at work on time just like Tanner had promised. And to her dizzying shock, her time with Tanner hadn't stopped the world from turning or her witness from being in the conference room so they could go over trial prep. Putting Tanner and her feelings for him out of her mind for now, she dove into work.

TANNER AND SCARLETT drove to his sister's house, a small house in Bayside, a well-kept home with little land but a lot of love inside. Alyssa and Nick had made the best of her getting pregnant unexpectedly and stayed together, falling in love over time and raising a great kid.

When he'd told Scarlett he wanted her to meet his sister, he hadn't been kidding. With his feelings for her growing by the day, he intended to do everything he could to ingrain her deeper into his life. It was the only way he could see her opening herself up to the possibility of a real future with him.

Because of what he didn't have growing up – the kind of family his sister now had – since meeting Scarlett, Tanner realized he could envision that for himself. Scarlett in his house, his bed, his life. The mother of his kids. Too bad he had no idea if she'd ever considered the idea of becoming a mom, or even getting married. Hell, he'd barely thought of it himself.

He glanced over at her pretty profile as he parked in front of his sister's place. Until now.

"We're here," he said unnecessarily, parking behind an idling navy car.

She'd surprised him by picking up flowers during a break she never usually took, to give to his sister for having her over. "Ready."

They headed up the walk just as the door opened and his nephew, Cal, barreled out and down the two steps outside, a duffel bag in his hand. "Uncle Tanner!"

"Hey!" He wrapped an arm around the boy's neck and pulled him in for as much of a hug as he'd allow these days. "Cal, this is Scarlett Davis. Scarlett, my nephew, Cal."

She smiled at the teen. "Hi. Nice to meet you."

"Where are you off to?" Tanner asked.

"The soccer team is having a sleepover at Steven's house. Joe's mom is waiting for me." He pointed to the navy car Tanner had seen earlier. "Are we still going to a Mets game soon?" He looked at Tanner with big brown eyes.

"You bet." He had a customer at the club with a high-up position on the team who could score him tickets. He'd already made the call and would follow up on it this weekend.

"Great! See ya!" He ran down the small front lawn and flew into the back seat of the car.

Scarlett met his gaze, a grin on her face. "He's got his uncle's good looks."

"Careful," he warned her. "Or I might think you like me." He tapped her on the nose and laughed.

Before Scarlett could answer, though she did blush red, his sister cleared her throat. "Ahem. Are you two going to come inside?" Alyssa stood by the open front door, watching them with a huge grin on her face.

"Hey, Lyssie."

"Don't call me that," she muttered.

"It was my childhood name for her and she hates it," Tanner explained, then introduced the two women in his life.

Alyssa smiled, looking happy. "Nick's in the family room watching television. Why don't you join him," she said as she closed the door behind him. "Scarlett can keep me company in the kitchen. I just have a few things to finish."

Tanner narrowed his gaze. "No snooping," he warned his sister. "No prying."

Scarlett laughed. "I can handle myself."

"I know you can. I'm just making sure my big sister behaves."

Alyssa rolled her eyes. "Not a shot in hell. Now shoo. Go away."

Tanner glanced at Scarlett, looking for a sign she was uncomfortable, but she and his sister had already started for the kitchen, his sister talking a mile a minute.

Maybe he should have thought twice about bringing her, he mused, because Alyssa might scare his girl off for good. With a shake of his head, he strode into the family room to join his brother-in-law.

Chapter Nine

I N THE BRIEF second she'd met Cal, Scarlett had been charmed by his relationship with his uncle. It was obvious the teen loved Tanner and wanted to spend time with him.

"Please, take a seat. I'm just going to get the salad ready," Alyssa, a pretty, dark-haired woman with similar features to Tanner, said as she pulled ingredients from the refrigerator.

"Can I help?"

Alyssa shook her head. "No thanks. I've got this down to a science. I haven't told Tanner yet but I'm going back to school to be a nurse. So I've learned to chop and dice quickly if we're going to have home-cooked meals and get me to class on time."

"That's wonderful! He's going to be so happy for you."

She smiled. "It's never too late to fulfill your dreams. I've gotten Cal to the self-sufficient point after school and Nick can pick him up after practice. We're good."

"I understand dreams," Scarlett murmured.

"What do you do?" Alyssa asked as she began to separate the lettuce, rip it into pieces, and throw it in the bowl.

Scarlett shifted in her seat, getting more comfortable. "I'm an assistant district attorney in Manhattan."

"Seriously? My brother and an ADA?"

A wry smile tipped Scarlett's lips. "They say opposites attract, right?" she said in an attempt to explain her and Tanner's unexpected connection.

Alyssa stared at her intently. "Okay, so Tanner didn't tell me ... anything about you two. He just said he was bringing a guest. But," she said before Scarlett could get a word in edgewise, "he's never brought anyone here before, never expressed interest in anyone, and that tells me something without him explaining."

Scarlett didn't think it was smart to mention that Tanner was sticking by her side until Victor Clark was caught and proven to be behind the various happenings at the club, and clearly Alyssa had already drawn her own conclusions. It was up to Tanner to give her the details of their relationship or at least his take on it.

"We're fairly new," she said. Although she felt like she had a good handle on who Tanner Grayson really was.

Although she'd moved from the lettuce on to the

tomatoes, chopping with proficiency, Alyssa paused to glance at Scarlett. "But he looked pretty taken with you, at least to me. And you're here." She placed the knife down on the counter and leaned toward the table where Scarlett sat. "My brother has been through a lot in his life. He's been hurt. I can tell you mean something to him, but if you're not as invested…"

Scarlett glanced from the knife to the other woman's intense stare. "Is this where you warn me not to hurt him or I'll have to answer to you?"

"Something like that. I just don't want to see him taken advantage of when he finally opens his heart."

Scarlett sat up straighter in her seat. "Your sentiments are in the right place, but the fact is, you don't know me enough to make assumptions. Tanner and I can work out our relationship ourselves. So can we call a truce and just enjoy our evening?"

She wanted to stay on this woman's good side because she meant so much to Tanner, but she wouldn't be bullied either. Even if she respected why Alyssa felt the need to play protective older sister.

"And it's a good thing I decided to come check on you ladies," Tanner said, stepping into the room. "Two strong-willed women. One who thinks she has to protect me from the world." He narrowed his gaze at his sister. "News flash. I can take care of myself. And whatever is between Scarlett and me? Is, as she

165

said, between Scarlett and me. Got it?" he asked Alyssa as he picked up a tomato and popped it into his mouth.

Although Scarlett didn't need him coming to her defense, she sensed he'd needed to assert himself with his sister, so she let him without argument.

"Point taken." Not even fazed by Tanner's reprimand, Alyssa nodded at him and met Scarlett's gaze. "But I like her." Her face changed with a warm, genuine smile. "And she's right. We should enjoy our evening." She tossed the ingredients in the bowl, adding dressing. "Dinner's ready."

And Scarlett, who was used to assertive people in her job, realized she'd passed whatever test and issues Alyssa might have had with her, and her shoulders lowered in relief. Although she hadn't come here thinking she'd have to earn her right to be in Tanner's life, Scarlett was glad he had a sister who cared enough to look out for him.

She often wondered, if her brother had lived, whether he'd have been protective and worried about the men she dated. If he'd insert himself in her life like Alyssa had just done. And she was sad she'd never get to find out.

"Scarlett? Are you okay?" Tanner now stood behind her, hand braced on the back of her chair, as he leaned close.

She blinked, realizing Alyssa had walked out of the room. "Yes. I'm fine. I was just … thinking of Hank," she said, deciding to be honest. "And wondering if he'd have looked out for me the way Alyssa does for you."

"My big sister is a pain in my ass. That said…" He kissed her forehead and met her gaze. "Hank would have vetted any guy who got close to you. And for sure he would have been proud of his sister."

Her throat filled and grew tight at his words. "Thank you," she whispered.

His warm grin caused her heart to skip a beat. "No, thank you, for putting up with Alyssa's shit. I'll talk to her so she doesn't pull a stunt like that again."

Scarlett waved away his statement. "No need. I think she and I have come to an understanding. Besides, I like her too."

Relief filled his expression and a definite sense of happiness lit up his eyes. "Ready to go join them in the dining room?"

She laughed and let him pull her up from her seat.

The rest of the evening passed as if the four of them were old friends. Alyssa asked a lot of questions about Scarlett's job as she obviously tried to get to know her better. Having made her sisterly point, she'd moved on. And Scarlett was happy to do so. She liked Nick, Alyssa's husband, and Alyssa broke her nursing school news over dessert. It turned into a celebratory night.

Later, they'd said goodbye, and she and Tanner agreed to stop by the club instead of going straight home. Scarlett didn't want to keep Tanner from his business completely, and it was the weekend, after all.

He parked his SUV behind the building, beside a Mercedes and a Jaguar, and helped her out of her side of the car. They walked hand in hand. Just as they turned the corner leading to the front entrance to the club, someone called Tanner's name.

He stiffened and turned slowly.

"Grayson!" a man called out a second time, as if he hadn't acknowledged him fast enough.

Following his lead, Scarlett spun around. And came face-to-face with Victor Clark.

Tanner's hand squeezed tighter around hers. "Go inside," he said in a rough voice.

As if she'd leave him alone with this man.

Victor, a large man with an evil, cold look in his eyes, still managed to appear pleased to see them. "It's been a long time," he said, shoving his hands into his jacket pockets.

"Not long enough," Tanner said through clenched teeth.

Scarlett ran her palm over his knuckles, trying to calm him by sheer touch.

"What are you doing here?" he asked.

Victor shrugged. "It's a free country, even for me. I can come and go as I please. I like checking out how well you've done for yourself. It shows me how far you can fall."

Oh, this man was slick. He didn't issue a direct threat yet he managed to make his words sound like a warning anyway.

"Get the fuck out of here," Tanner growled.

"Make me." Victor took a step forward, obviously taunting Tanner.

And Tanner's entire body vibrated with a combination of anger and tension. He'd released his hold on her and had his hands balled into tight fists.

Her stomach churned and she glanced over her shoulder, but no one was in sight. She wished she could go find one of his partners inside, but she refused to leave him alone with Victor.

"No? Not going to take a swing? You've learned to control that nasty temper of yours? We'll see how long that lasts." He turned his gaze from Tanner to Scarlett. "Nice to see you again, Ms. Davis."

Tanner pulled her roughly against him.

"How do you know who I am?" she asked.

Even his smile frightened her. "I make it my business to know everything about the men who put me away. Even their side pieces."

A low growl sounded from Tanner's throat. "She has nothing to do with history, Vic. Leave her out of it."

"Out of what?" he asked with fake innocence.

"Cut the bullshit. Everything you've done around here. What's your endgame?"

Victor shrugged. "Afraid I don't know what you're talking about. But if you've got problems, maybe you just have more enemies than you know what to do with." He chuckled, the sound low and menacing.

"Lying sack of—"

Tanner rolled back on his heels and Scarlett feared he'd let loose any second.

"What's going on?" Landon's voice reverberated through the dark night.

A glance told Scarlett that Jason and the big, bald bodyguard was with him, and relief filled her at the sight of them.

His gaze landed on Vic. "What the fuck are you doing here?"

"Taking a walk and talking to an old *friend*. Now excuse me. I have somewhere to be." And just like that, he turned and walked away, leaving Tanner seething beside her.

She'd never seen him like this, eyes glittering with anger, unable to really see anything but the opponent he viewed in front of him. She wasn't worried for herself. She wasn't scared of Tanner. She was scared *for* him.

✧   ✧   ✧

TANNER BARELY REMEMBERED how they'd gotten from the street to the office, where Jason shoved a glass of Scotch into his hand. "Drink. You need it to calm down."

Aware of everyone's eyes on him, including Scarlett, he accepted the amber liquid and pulled a long sip, letting the burn make its way down his chest as he focused on breathing slowly and steadily.

"How did you know to come outside?" Scarlett, who was sitting on the sofa on the other side of the room from Tanner, asked.

"Video cameras. Every time something happens, we install another one so we don't miss a damn thing."

"You did good," Jason told Tanner. "Kept your temper in check, talked but didn't go after him."

"Don't fucking patronize me," he said, hating feeling weak in front of anyone but particularly Scarlett, whose opinion of him mattered most.

He'd been going out of his way to show her the man he was today and fucking Victor arrived and all Tanner could see was a haze of anger in front of him.

"Just telling it like I see it."

Scarlett rose and walked over to him, hesitantly, as

if unsure of him. "Tanner, he's right. You didn't let him goad you into a fight. That's what he wanted. You didn't give him that." Taking him by surprise, she wrapped her arms around his waist and put her head on his shoulder. "Can we go home?" she asked softly.

Relaxing for the first time since he'd seen Vic, he shifted so he was holding her in his arms. "Just a few more minutes." He glanced at the guys. "So?"

"So nothing. Yet. But we've got a guy watching Sutherland's home and his club. If Vic shows up there, at least we'll have our connection. Because we know Daniel was involved at least with the initial vandalism. What we don't know is at what point Vic stepped in."

Tanner nodded. "Keep me posted. We're leaving."

Jason stood up and walked over. "You okay?"

He nodded. "Come on." He took Scarlett's hand and they headed home.

In the car, he remained silent and she respected his withdrawal. Once at the house, he set the alarm. He wasn't taking any chances.

A little while later, he'd washed up and climbed into bed. He knew better than to think he could sleep. Scarlett joined him, sliding between the sheets, smelling fruity and sweet.

"You smell good." And in her pale pink satiny camisole that hit her mid-thigh, she looked even better.

She grinned. "When I picked up flowers for your sister, I also stopped at the pharmacy and grabbed some toiletries for me. I hope you don't mind, but you're now officially sharing your bathroom with a woman ... with all the little bottles and things that entails."

As long as the items belonged to her, he was good. But how was she feeling after what she'd witnessed tonight? He might have kept his cool to an outside observer, but inside he'd been a mess, and he knew Scarlett was observant enough to have noticed.

"Hey." She pushed herself over to his side of the bed, picked up his arm, and put it around her, then rested her head on his chest. "You're miles away and I don't like it."

Unable to help himself, he relaxed and let her cuddle up against him. His dick reacted but that wasn't what he wanted or needed from her tonight.

"What did you see tonight? In me? When dealing with Victor?" he asked her.

She stiffened at the question, then took her time answering. "I saw ... a man struggling to maintain control and not lose his temper or let his anger get the best of him. I also saw a man who accomplished all of those things."

"What you didn't see was the haze of anger inside me. If he'd pushed just the right button, I'm afraid I might have gone off on him." He admitted the truth out loud because she deserved to hear it from him before getting involved. Or more involved, as they case might be.

She sighed, her hands trailing over his bare chest. "So you're a work in progress in that area. The important thing is you're aware. And you know what you have to lose. I think you need to trust yourself more. The guys do."

But did she? He wasn't ready to ask.

"We all have our challenges. The key is how we rise to face them." Tanner nodded in agreement.

Somehow this amazing woman was in his life and he'd do everything he could to keep her there. He only hoped his best was good enough and the past didn't keep returning to threaten the present.

ONE WEEK AFTER running into Vic, and Tanner was finished with the self-pitying attitude. In the days that had passed, he took a step back and really looked at himself and how he'd behaved with his biggest enemy, the one person capable of sending him over the edge and potentially causing him to ruin his own life. Because if Victor's actions got to him, Tanner had no one to blame but himself.

He also thought back to his talk with Scarlett and

let her words wash over him. She hadn't said she saw a man free of his behavior, she'd said she saw a man working on controlling it. And she was right. He was working ... and succeeding, Vic be damned.

But they had a bigger problem than Vic at this moment. The bomb threat had affected their bottom line, customers obviously uncertain about returning. They were going to have to work to bring their patrons back, and Tanner, along with his partners, was pissed. In particular, Tanner wasn't as red-hazy angry with Vic as he was fucking determined to turn things around. His sole focus was and always would be the club and not the asshole causing trouble, although he had every intention of making him pay.

He called the guys together late in the day while Scarlett was at work and he could meet at the club without disrupting her schedule.

"I have an idea," he said to them. "One that will take a lot of money for security but it'll definitely bring the customers back in." He'd stayed up all night thinking and he finally realized what they needed to do.

"I'm listening," Landon said.

"Same." Jason walked to the fridge, pulled out bottles of water, and tossed one to each of them.

"How did we put ourselves on the map with live entertainment?" Tanner asked the men.

They glanced at each other.

"Lola and Charlotte's opening-night performance," Jason said, his voice rising with excitement.

Tanner nodded. "Right. So what if we bring in an equally big draw? Announce it soon and give people a chance to see, get excited, and come back to the club?"

"Got anyone in mind?" Landon asked.

Tanner looked to Jason. "Grey Kingston. Your brother-in-law couldn't make it last time but maybe he can now." His wife, Avery, Jason's half sister, had found out she was pregnant and her first trimester had been a bitch. She was further along now so hopefully Grey wouldn't mind coming for a performance.

Jason rubbed a hand over his face, as he thought. "Grey seemed disappointed he couldn't make it last time. I think he'd enjoy coming back for a one-shot performance since he usually writes songs and hasn't been on stage in a while." He let out a low hum. "I wonder if the old band would get back together with him."

Grey had been part of the rock band Tangled Royal with Lola Corbin, who'd already performed at their opening night. Ultimately Grey had grown tired of the road, retired, and the band went their own way. But Grey had pull. He could get the band back if he wanted to.

"I like it," Tanner said, excitement pulsing in his

veins.

"It's a solid idea. I'll give Grey a call," Jason said. "But I want this shit wrapped up and a lock on Vic before we bring in big talent."

Tanner nodded. "Agreed. My gut tells me Vic is gearing up for something. He's not going to be satisfied just toying with us. He wants to destroy us." His stomach churned at the thought.

"Then we need to make sure if we can't outsmart him in advance, that we can at least be ready when whatever it is hits," Tanner said. "How about we talk to Sutherland? Owner to owner? See what he has to say? Because somehow there has to be a link between them. It doesn't make sense that they'd both be targeting the club."

Landon nodded. "It's too close to opening tonight to pay the man a visit now, but what if we plan to go over there first thing in the morning?"

"Agreed." Tanner and Jason spoke at the same time.

"Meanwhile I'll call Grey and get a date set up. Then we can work on publicity," Jason said.

"Perfect. Now, if you'll excuse me, I have a woman to pick up from work." Tanner stood and started for the door.

Scarlett had told him to wear a jacket tonight when he picked her up, which left him confused. But far be it for him to deny her. He'd stop upstairs and change on his way out.

"I like her for you," Jason said as Tanner's hand reached for the doorknob.

He glanced over his shoulder at his friend. "I like her for me too."

He just didn't have a handle on her feelings on the relationship or the future. He knew she felt something for him but he also understood she was allowing this time away from work because of the threat. When Vic was back behind bars where he belonged and Tanner didn't have an excuse to be by her side, would she pull away again?

Or could he convince her to make permanent time in her life for a real relationship? The kind she tended to avoid.

AS HARD AS it was for Scarlett to admit, she looked forward to Tanner's arrival at night to take her home to his house. As the clock ticked down, she packed up her things and was ready to leave when Tanner showed up in her doorway.

"Looks like someone is ready and waiting for me." He leaned against the frame, his broad shoulders and large presence a sexy sight.

"I am."

"And are you going to tell me why I'm dressed up?" He fingered the lapels of his black jacket that had obviously been tailored just for him.

She smiled. "I have a surprise for you." She'd worked hard all week for this moment.

He raised an eyebrow and stepped into the room, coming up to her and pulling her into his arms. "Yeah? What's that?"

She inhaled his seductive masculine scent. Unable to help herself, she leaned in and pressed her nose against his neck, nuzzling her lips there but really giving herself a better whiff and taste. The man was delicious. "I'm taking you out for dinner. To a nice restaurant. No rushed takeout or delivery."

"No work from home tonight?"

She understood the question. She did a lot of work in bed surrounded by file folders and her laptop and he was always patient about it, never complaining. "Not tonight. I'm all yours."

He grinned and kissed her lips. "Let's go."

She further surprised him by taking them to Daniel, a five-star restaurant on Sixty-Fifth Street, where she'd pulled strings and gotten them a reservation. Chef Daniel Boulud had opened an eatery with a fabulous wine cellar and stellar reputation for French and European cuisine.

They each had a delicious meal of grilled swordfish

and butternut squash and wine recommended by the sommelier. Tanner eyed her warmly throughout the meal, his eyes always focused on her, and they talked about easy, comfortable things. Nothing heavy or serious. They just enjoyed.

Tonight clearly meant something to him and she was glad. He deserved to feel special. He'd made her feel that way often enough, and after all he'd gone through with Vic, she wanted him to know she viewed him as someone worthy and important.

The waiter handed them the dessert menu and stepped away so they could decide.

"I want something chocolate," she murmured, determined not to miss a course in this fabulous restaurant.

He chuckled, reaching across the table and lacing his fingers with hers. "Whatever you want."

She ordered a pecan infused chocolate dish with salted caramel praline that tasted even better than it looked if such a thing were possible.

She held out her spoon for Tanner to try. He opened his mouth and wrapped those talented lips around the dessert, closing his eyes as he sampled the treat. "Mmm."

Her body reacted to the sexy sound, her panties dampening as he groaned in delight.

"Fucking delicious," he muttered.

She grinned. "Isn't it?"

His eyes darkened. "Not as good as you taste, but definitely second-best."

She laughed and wagged a finger at him. "Dirty man."

He shrugged. "What can I say? You make me crazy."

She leaned closer but there was still a table between them. She couldn't wait to get home and let him do what he was alluding to. Then she could taste him too.

His gaze never left hers and she could see the desire in his eyes and his expression. Until the sound of his cell phone interrupted the moment.

He frowned at the unwanted noise and hit his phone, ending the call without checking it. Until the ring sounded again.

"I'm sorry." He held up a finger and pulled out his phone, frowning as he looked at the screen. He answered the call. "Jason, it's a really bad time."

She waited not so patiently to find out what his partner wanted.

"Say that again?" Tanner listened, his eyes opening in disbelief. "I'll be right there." He disconnected the call and slammed the phone onto the table. "A raid. A fucking police raid because there've been reports that we serve underage kids."

Anger and disbelief rushed through her. "That's ridiculous."

He gestured for the check.

"Don't kill me but it's already covered. I left my credit card when I made the reservation."

He narrowed his gaze at her. "Why?"

"Because I wanted to take you out. I wanted to reciprocate for all you've done for me, but mostly I wanted you to know that you're a special man." She reached out and touched his hand. "I'm just sorry it ended this way."

She'd planned a much different finale at home in bed. She'd even bought a new nightie for the occasion. She sighed, knowing she wouldn't get use out of that garment tonight.

He drew a deep breath and smiled. "Thank you, beautiful. That means a lot."

They spoke to the waiter, she placed her napkin on the table, and they rushed out.

Chapter Ten

TANNER SWEAT AS they sat in a dark, dingy room at the police station answering questions. He'd sent Scarlett home with one of the bodyguards from the club, leaving the man with instructions to walk her inside, wait until she set the alarm, and not to leave the grounds until Tanner returned.

The memories this interrogation brought back were not good ones. Him, barely an adult, sitting without a lawyer as the cops yelled questions at him from across the table. Until Jason called Gabe and sent Thomas Culhane to bail him out. The man was now a friend and still their lawyer.

Jason had already called him, and the man had met them there, sitting by their side during the interrogation about how they ran their business.

"What gives you the right to haul my clients in on a so-called tip?" Tommy asked.

The lead detective slid a picture across the table. "We have a photo of someone who's underage and was served at your club. And we have reason to believe he's not the only one."

"I happen to know we're vigilant," Landon said. "This is bullshit."

Tanner picked up the photo of a New York State driver's license. Although it was grainy, he studied it because the young man in the picture looked familiar. "How do we know him?" He slid the paper to Landon.

His friend lifted the sheet and studied it. "That bastard!"

"Wait." Tommy glanced at the detectives. "I want a word alone with my clients."

With a nod, the two men left the room.

"What is it?" Tommy, who'd been thirty when he bailed Tanner out, was now a decade older with even more experience behind him. And he was good. They kept him on retainer.

"This kid." Landon pointed to the photo. "He's one of the kids we caught vandalizing our patrons' cars. He said Daniel Sutherland, who owns Club Zero downtown, paid them cash to destroy some cars in our back lot and scare people from returning to the club."

Tommy glared at each man for a long second. "And you didn't report this to the cops?"

"We got the information we wanted. We didn't want to ruin a couple of idiot kids' lives. We gave them a good warning and sent them on their way," Tanner muttered.

Tommy groaned. "Look, Tanner. I'm guessing you saw yourself in those kids and you let them off the hook."

He ducked his head because he had. Oh, he so had. And he didn't want those young kids sitting behind bars without a Gabriel Dare, Jason, and Landon to save them.

"Okay, we'll go from here." Tommy placed the photo on the table.

"We have security cameras everywhere in the club. If they have a date and time on this kid showing up at the club, we can prove the bartender proofed him," Jason said.

Tommy nodded. "I'll explain all this to the cops. And we'll send them to Sutherland. Let them squeeze him for information."

Tanner wanted to get to Daniel himself, first. Talk man to man and have him give up Vic as his accomplice. But he didn't want to play games with the police either and piss them off. "Fine."

Tommy glanced from Jason to Landon, who agreed. "Yeah. Okay."

An hour later, because the wheels of justice turned slowly and the police station operated even more slowly, they were let go with a warning they might be called in for further questioning. But they hadn't been arrested.

Exhausted, Tanner headed back to the now empty club with his partners, where they gathered around the bar. They sat in heavy silence until suddenly the front door opened, causing everyone to stiffen.

"Who's there?" Tanner called out.

"Hold your fire," a familiar voice jokingly said, as Daniel Sutherland walked inside, hands up in front of him.

Tanner blinked. "What the fuck are you doing here?"

Jason placed a hand on his shoulder. "What do you want, Sutherland?"

He strode over, pulled up a stool, and sat down.

"Join us, why don't you," Landon muttered.

"I heard you guys had a raid tonight." The man ran a hand over his perfectly styled blond hair.

Tanner narrowed his gaze. "On a tip you called in?"

Sutherland scowled. "Frankly, no. Though I can see why you'd think so."

"Look, we've had a long fucking night. Did you come here for a reason or just to shoot the shit?" Tanner asked. Before they broached the subject of Victor Clark, he wanted to hear what the other club owner had to say.

The man hung his head and groaned. "I targeted

you, okay? You guys opened up and took business away from me. So I hired a couple of punk kids to cause some trouble. It wasn't well thought out, but I panicked that I wouldn't be able to pay my bills."

Tanner looked at the man, unimpressed with his reasoning. "Yeah? A bomb scare sounded like a good idea to you? In this day and age?"

Daniel shook his head hard. "Fuck no. That's when I was out. I would never go along with something like that. It's too fucking dangerous and the penalty if I'm caught? It's a federal offense! I'm not spending a decade or more in jail!"

The man's panic sounded real and Tanner met his friends' gazes.

"Okay, so what's going on? From the beginning, okay?" Jason strode up to Sutherland, getting into his personal space.

Sutherland rubbed his palms against his eyes, then blinked and met Tanner's gaze. "My brother was in prison with Victor Clark."

Fucking BINGO.

"Victor protected my brother. Pulled him in and let it be known not to touch him. And my brother's a scrawny guy and they would have had it out for him inside." Daniel cringed, then glanced at Landon, who stood behind the bar. "Got a drink?" he asked.

Scowling, Landon picked up a bottle of cheap

scotch and filled a glass, sliding it toward Sutherland, who downed half of it in one gulp.

"So you owed Vic." Tanner wanted the whole story out there.

"Yeah. And when he got out of prison, he showed up on my doorstep, wanting that debt repaid. He had looked into your club. Knew we were competitors. I'd already pulled the stupid shit, hacking your sound system and vandalizing patrons' cars. Vic wanted to target you without getting caught, so he demanded I continue what I'd started."

"Go on." Tanner ground his teeth together.

"I hit up your cars. I mean, I hired someone to do it. But I guess Victor was impatient and he wanted bigger things to happen. He didn't say why and I didn't ask, but he pulled the bomb scare himself behind my back. And then I was *out*." He held up both hands, like he was swearing, then downed the rest of the liquor. "I told him not to come back but he's been threatening me. Meanwhile I heard you guys were taken in tonight and I couldn't live with myself. So here I am."

Thank God, Tanner thought, thumping his hand on the bar. This mess would all be over soon, and with parole violations thanks to illegal behavior and a bomb threat under his belt, Victor was going back to prison for a long fucking time.

"Call Tommy," Tanner said. "Let's do this the legal way." He blew out a relieved breath because Victor Clark would soon be out of his life for good.

It was late, nearing morning, when Tanner waved off the security guard outside his home and let himself into the house. Exhaustion pulled at him and he couldn't wait to crawl into bed and pass out.

He stepped into his room and realized Scarlett had left the light on in the bathroom with the door cracked open. Catching sight of her asleep in his bed, he grinned. Her blonde hair flowed over the pillow and she didn't move when he walked in.

Not only could he get used to this in his future, he already had. Unfortunately, once Victor was arrested, Scarlett would have no reason to remain in his house and in his bed. She could go back to her life, living in the city and making her easy commute to the office. The thought churned his stomach.

He undressed, taking off all his clothes and crawling into bed, his muscles and bones screaming in gratitude the minute the soft mattress enveloped him. But he wasn't ready to sleep until he slid to the middle of the bed and pulled Scarlett into his arms, wrapped his big body around hers, and then he let himself crash. Hard.

✧ ✧ ✧

SCARLETT MOANED AND shifted her hips restlessly against the bed, desire flooding her veins as the most delicious sensation gathered between her thighs. At first she thought she was dreaming, and if so, she didn't want to wake up. Not when a talented tongue was lapping at her sex and teeth were grazing her clit with a touch so light it was like a spark was lit and faded before she could grab on to it and fly.

She opened her eyes, glanced at the ceiling, and the sensations continued. Nope, not asleep.

She spread her legs wider. "Tanner."

"Hmm." He hummed against her sex and she arched her hips, needing more friction. More pressure. Just more.

"Come up here," she murmured. She wanted his cock inside her, his mouth on her lips.

"Uh-uh. Not until you come."

And how could she argue with that logic?

He set to work, devouring her like a starving man, licking and sucking until she was soaring, her orgasm overtaking her without warning. And before she could come back to herself, he'd lifted himself up and over her and thrust deep inside. Her body readily accepted him, but instead of the hard thrusting she was used to from him, he rocked against her, slowly taking her higher.

He met her gaze and she felt the magnetic pull,

unable to look away as she clasped him tighter, heard him groan, stiffen, and come, filling her with his essence, his climax triggering another one of her own.

A little while later, cleaned up, she lay in the crook of his arm. "What happened at the police station?"

She'd been nervous when the police officers insisted on taking the three partners to the precinct, but she'd let Tanner send her home because he'd assured her they had a good lawyer on the way. As an ADA, she could have accompanied them, but she handled bigger, more complex cases and she had a hunch her presence would only complicate things. The guys seemed to have it under control.

"I tried to stay up but I obviously didn't make it," she said regretfully.

He groaned. "I got back late." His fingers tangled in her hair as he spoke. "The cops thought they had a case against us for letting underage kids drink. They had a photo of a license of someone they say we served. But we recognized him as one of the vandals of our patrons' cars. So it sounds like a setup."

She didn't like any of this.

"The security company is pulling footage. I'm sure our bartenders proofed the kid. But whoever called the precinct made it sound like it was an ongoing habit." He frowned. "It's not."

"I know." She placed her hand over his chest, feeling his heartbeat and taking comfort in touching him. "Are you in trouble?"

He shook his head. "We shouldn't be." He pushed himself up against the headboard, resettling her against his chest. "And we had an interesting visitor last night. Daniel Sutherland, the competitor we know was targeting us, admitted his connection to Vic."

"You're kidding!" She tipped her head up and met his gaze.

"Nope. The idea of a bomb threat charge had him shaking, and when he heard about the raid last night … he came forward. He says Vic was acting on his own at the end."

"Do you believe him?" she asked.

"Yeah." He didn't hesitate. "Vic's a loose cannon. Always was."

"Does that mean the threat is over?" She held her breath, uncertain how she felt about that because the end result of Vic's arrest would mean she had no reason to be with Tanner all the time. Forced togetherness would end and she could go back to her life.

The one she'd prided herself on. The one she thought she lived for. The one that left her no time for anything … or anyone else. Her heart hurt at the thought, taking her off guard.

"No." He squeezed her tighter. "Absolutely not. Until the cops hear about Vic, verify and act on the information, then take him into custody, nothing here changes. We're careful and vigilant."

She nodded, snuggling closer, letting out a relieved breath. She still had time before she had to think about what happened between her and Tanner when the threat to them came to an end.

✦　✦　✦

TANNER ACCOMPANIED SCARLETT to visit her mother at the home where she'd been admitted. Although he could have sent Scarlett with a bodyguard, Tanner knew their time together was counting down, and he wanted to make the most of what little they had left.

As they walked toward the room, her father stepped out and smiled when he saw them. "Hi! I'm happy you're here."

"Thanks, Dad. How is she?" Scarlett asked.

"The same, unfortunately. She's recovered from the carbon monoxide poisoning but her depression is status quo." He glanced toward her mother's door and sighed.

Tanner squeezed Scarlett's hand for support.

"Did you make a decision about ECT treatment?" Scarlett asked her father.

The other man nodded. "Although she doesn't talk much, your mother is adamant that she doesn't want it. She shakes her head no whenever the subject comes up." He paused. "I'm going to respect her wishes. Especially since the side effects aren't good. Memory loss, confusion, high blood pressure, which she already has. In addition, it takes a series of treatments, and in my heart, I don't think it's right for her."

Tanner glanced at Scarlett, who appeared sad but resigned.

"I respect your decision, Dad. I'd probably make the same one myself." She stepped forward and hugged her father. "I wouldn't blame you if you started living your own life, either. You've done everything you can for her. Visit when you want to but ... don't give up living because she has."

Tears formed in her father's eyes and Tanner felt like an intruder on a very intimate family conversation. He'd take a step away but that would be too obvious, so he remained silent, watching the moment between father and daughter, his heart going out to them both.

"That's the most generous thing you've ever said to me," Mack said.

She blinked and a tear fell from her eyes too. "I guess I've started to see what living really means lately." She glanced over her shoulder at Tanner and gave him a small smile. One that made his stomach twist in a really positive way. "And I'd hate for you to waste the rest of your life not enjoying it."

A regretful look crossed Mack's face. "I wish I

could say I raised you right, but I didn't have much to do with it, did I? I worked a lot and your mother wasn't really around. Then Hank died and you were always alone…"

She shook her head. "I was fine. As fine as I could be anyway. Can we just move forward from here?"

God, his girl was strong, Tanner thought. He wanted nothing more than to gather her into his arms and prevent anything bad from hurting her. But for now, all he could do was stand by her side for as long as she let him.

Her father nodded in gratitude.

"I'm going to see Mom." Scarlett drew a deep breath and walked into the room, leaving Tanner with Mack Davis.

"Let's walk," the older man said.

With a nod, Tanner strode down the carpeted hall, Scarlett's father by his side. The low murmur of televisions sounded from rooms as they passed, but he couldn't deny the depressive feeling of the place.

"So … you and my daughter."

Tanner drew his shoulders straighter. "Yes, sir."

"Is it serious? I mean, I assume any man accompanying a woman to her mother's bedside after a suicide scare and to see her in a mental hospital has good intentions."

Tanner grinned, actually appreciating the fact that

her father was looking out for her. Although it might come late, it wasn't too late to fix what was broken between them. So he didn't take offense to the question. Hell, if he had a daughter, he'd be all over any man who came near her, making sure he treated his baby right. And he suddenly realized how badly he wanted that. With Scarlett.

"Yes, I do. The best of intentions. Although I'm not certain your daughter wants the same things I do."

Mack stopped at the window at the far end of the hall. "My daughter didn't have a solid example of a good marriage. She raised herself and she's scared of opening her heart. Are you the type to give up when the going gets tough?"

Tanner met Mack Davis's gaze. "No." He definitely wasn't a quitter. And in the last couple of weeks, he'd come to recognize his own self-worth, in large part thanks to how Scarlett viewed him. Yeah, his partners had always tried to tell him the same things she did. But it took Vic's return to show him he was a man in control of his actions and his destiny.

"Well, that's good to know. Take care of my girl, Mr. Grayson."

"Tanner," he said. "And I intend to do just that." As long as she let him.

✧   ✧   ✧

THE WEEK BEGAN with hope, Tanner and the guys hoping the cops acted on their information. Tommy promised to stay on top of them and keep everyone informed of how the police intended to handle Sutherland and Vic.

As far as the club was concerned, Jason not only lined up Grey Kingston, but he'd secured a reunion of Tangled Royal. The publicist in charge of the club took off running with the information … holding out on the date of the event. Only those in the know understood they were waiting for Vic's arrest to announce when. It was everyone's priority to keep the customers and the band safe.

But Tanner's hope quickly evaporated regarding Vic. Yes, the cops spoke to Daniel Sutherland and knew they were after Victor Clark, but he'd disappeared. According to Sutherland, he didn't know where Vic had been staying, but he did have a cell phone number for him … that turned out to be to a burner phone.

Vic was nowhere to be found.

Meanwhile, life went on. Faith asked them to throw a surprise party for Jason at the club, and they picked a Wednesday night so as not to interfere with the weekend rush and so the crowd would be smaller at the club. In other words, so they could fit more Dares into one room.

Jason had a massively huge family. First, he had two full siblings and six half siblings, all married, not to mention three cousins who lived in New York. Most of the family resided in the Miami Beach, Florida, area but his sister Sienna and her husband, Ethan Knight, lived in Manhattan. Ethan had three siblings, two of whom were in the city ... and on and on.

It made Tanner's head spin. Especially when the Florida siblings, half and full, along with Jason's mother, Savannah, and her new boyfriend, decided to make a trip to celebrate Jason's thirtieth birthday.

It was Faith's job to bring Jason to the club on his day off for the surprise. She had, of course, created lots of candy pops and other delicious treats for the occasion and dropped them off earlier in the day.

Scarlett made a huge fuss about picking out an appropriate dress for the party, finally choosing a sexy but sophisticated black number that she brought to work to change into before Tanner picked her up to head over to the club.

When he arrived, he took one look at her and nearly swallowed his tongue. Her hair fell over her shoulders in disarray, her makeup had been freshened, and that dress dipped low between her luscious breasts, teasing him with just a hint of cleavage. Classy, sexy, and all his, at least for the time being.

"Hi, gorgeous."

She grinned when she looked up and saw him standing there. "Hi, yourself, handsome." She rose and came around her desk, this time revealing her long legs and high-heeled black pumps.

He wanted those legs wrapped around his waist. Now. And he wondered if anyone would notice if he shut the door and bent her over her desk. Then he could spend the rest of the evening all but pounding his chest like a caveman because his woman smelled like him when she talked to other men.

"Tanner? I asked if you were ready to leave. You spaced out. Everything okay?"

He chuckled, for damn sure not planning to reveal his thoughts. "It's all good. You all set?"

She nodded. "I'm even leaving work here and not taking anything home tonight. Has Jason's family arrived?"

He'd tried to give her a rundown of all the names and spouses, but her eyes had glazed over and he didn't blame her. She'd meet them all in person soon.

"They're at the club. And Jason is picking Faith up at the shop, stopping home so she can change for a nice dinner for his birthday. Landon's going to call with an *emergency*," he said, gesturing with air quotes. "And get him to the club for the surprise."

"Sounds well thought out." She picked up her

purse, a dressier one than the big bag she usually carried. "All set."

After they'd settled in the Uber – he hadn't seen the point in driving – she asked, "So no news?"

She didn't have to use Vic's name. They both knew who she meant.

He shook his head. "But life goes on and we're not going to stop our plans because the asshole is out there. We've got security, and his picture has been handed out to each guard."

"Okay. So we hang tight." He pulled her into him and they made their way downtown.

They hadn't shut down the club to outsiders, and thanks to the news of Tangled Royal coming to Club TEN29, customers had returned to the venue. Despite it being a Wednesday, between the regulars and Jason's friends and big, happy family, the place was packed.

Tanner walked around introducing Scarlett to the Dares he knew best. First up was Gabe and Izzy, a curvy brunette, with a warm, generous personality. "You've heard me mention Gabe Dare? This is the man himself and his wife, Isabelle."

"I've heard great things about you," Scarlett said to Gabe. "So nice to meet you." She smiled at Izzy.

They shared small talk, and then Tanner caught sight of Lucy Dare and her husband, Max Savage, and he called them over. "This is my decorator, Lucy Dare.

Lucy and Max, this is Scarlett."

And on and on it went until finally, Landon let out a whistle. "Just heard from Faith. They're parking and should be here any minute."

A little while later, Faith and Jason walked in the door and headed back toward the bar. "Surprise!" everyone called out.

"Let the party begin," Tanner whispered in Scarlett's ear.

She grinned. "Aww, Jason looks so shocked and happy to see his family."

They stayed for another couple of hours, mingled with Jason's family and friends, and ate Faith's delicious candy.

"Thanks for coming," Jason said, joining them by the end of the bar, where they'd gone for as much quiet as they could find in the crowded room.

"Happy birthday." Tanner slapped his friend on the back, then pulled him in for a brotherly hug.

"Happy birthday, Jason." Scarlett stepped over, lifted herself up onto her tiptoes, and kissed his cheek. "I hope you have a wonderful year."

"Did you have fun?" he asked Scarlett. "I know my family can be a bit much."

She laughed at that mild description. "I actually like them all. Not that I can keep everyone straight but I tried. It must be nice to have such a warm, loving family."

Jason shot a startled glance at Tanner.

"Sorry, man. I haven't had time to explain your crazy family dynamics to her." He glanced at her. "Let's just say it involves a cheating father, a second family, a bone marrow donation, and a big reveal. I'll explain in detail later."

Jason barked out a laugh. "That's the most succinct description ever. It's taken us all awhile to get to the point where we are now. All family and friends." He glanced out over the crowd. "But now? I'm grateful for them all."

Tanner knew that, like him, Scarlett felt the lack of family in her life. The pain of what she didn't have and the loss of those she loved.

"Sounds like a soap opera I'd love to hear," she said.

"I'll let him tell you. I'm going to find Faith. Thanks again, guys, and feel free to bail at any time." He winked at them.

Tanner chuckled. "I think we'll take him up on that. You ready?"

"Beyond. I'm exhausted."

They headed outside to Tanner's SUV.

"That was such an amazing party and I can't wait to hear Jason's family story," Scarlett said, going on about all the Dares she'd met, why she liked each one, who had exchanged phone numbers with her because they'd hit it off.

He listened to her happy voice as he opened the door for her, letting her in and closing it behind her. And because he was distracted by Scarlett and still thinking about the party, he missed the man hidden in the alley until he got the jump on him.

A large, strong arm came around Tanner's neck, pulling him into the shadows, cutting off his circulation and ability to fight back. "You are not going to fucking ruin my life again."

Vic. Tanner pulled at the arm, needing air flow.

To his shock, Vic released him, and Tanner stumbled before righting himself and facing the other man. "If I'm going down, you're going with me," Vic said, clearly wanting the fight Tanner was trying to avoid.

He breathed in deep, more in control of himself than he'd have expected. "How? I'd have to beat you bloody again and I'm not stupid enough to lose everything because of you." Even if now that hazy anger was threatening to overwhelm him, the voice of reason remained stronger.

"Yeah? What if I pull that pretty blonde out of the car and fuck her while you watch?"

Yeah. The red glow took over. He darted forward and grabbed Vic around the neck, pinning him against the wall. "Don't look at her. Don't touch her. Don't even think about her."

The son of a bitch grinned. "What do you say? Want to spread your legs for me, Scarlett?"

Tanner didn't think, he jerked his hand and Vic's head hit the wall.

"Tanner, no. This is what he wants!" Scarlett yelled from behind him and he realized she was watching.

Watching him turn into the angry animal Vic wanted him to become.

In the second she distracted him, Vic shook himself loose and came after Tanner with a swing to his jaw.

Scarlett screamed but Tanner couldn't allow himself to be taken off guard again. He didn't plan on getting himself tossed in jail for assault again, but he wasn't about to take the beating, either. He'd had enough MMA experience to go after Vic another way.

WHEN TANNER DIDN'T come right around to his side of the SUV, Scarlett realized something was wrong. She hopped out of the car to see Vic's arm around Tanner's neck, Tanner struggling for breath. In a heartbeat, the situation was reversed. Tanner had Vic against the wall.

Fear like she'd never known paralyzed her where she stood. Especially after Tanner shook Vic so hard he hit his head against the wall.

She wasn't strong enough to get between them, and she didn't want to run away to get help. She was afraid Tanner would kill Vic and then what? All the work he'd done to be a better man would be for nothing. But Vic knew that and was taunting Tanner, goading him, and using threats to Scarlett to do it. He wanted Tanner to bury himself with his anger.

When Vic freed himself and hit Tanner, Scarlett screamed and Tanner grappled with the man, pulling him to the ground. Unable to watch, she ran for help, barreling into the bar, screaming. But security must have already seen what was going on outside through their monitors because no sooner had she stepped in the door than the guys and the big bald guard ran past her, nearly knocking her down in the process.

She drew a deep, shaky breath. Part of her didn't want to go outside and see if Vic was bloody and beaten on the ground … or worse, if Tanner was. And another part of her, the part that knew Tanner deep in her soul, wanted to believe he wouldn't succumb to his darker impulses, not even with Vic.

"Scarlett?" Faith ran to her, wrapping an arm around her. "Honey, you're trembling. Come sit."

"But…" Her teeth *were* chattering. "Vic is outside and Tanner…" She could barely get the words out.

Faith eased her into a barstool. "I know. Security

came running down after they'd caught the fight on the live feed. It's going to be okay. The cops are on their way."

Faith glanced over at the bartender. "Give me a shot of whiskey."

He poured one and Faith handed Scarlett the glass. "Take a drink. Come on. You're going to be fine. Tanner is going to be fine."

"I know. I believe in him." In the instant when she'd seen him shake the man, she'd wavered. But in her heart, she knew. Tanner was solid. He was going to handle it right. As long as Vic didn't hurt him. "I just… I was scared. I'm still so scared."

Faith treated her to a grim smile. "I'd take you outside to see for yourself but Jason will turn my ass red," she said, not looking at all put out by the notion.

Her innocent eyelash batting let Scarlett relax and even laugh a little.

Then she took another drink and settled in to wait, because like Faith, if she showed her face outside before the police arrived, Tanner would lose his shit with worry. And she didn't want to distract him again.

Chapter Eleven

TANNER HAD VIC in a headlock by the time the guys showed up and their security guard, Glenn, took over. Between his gun and the cuffs he'd slapped on a shouting Vic, Tanner could finally breathe easily again.

He straightened his jacket and blew out a breath.

"You okay?" Landon placed a hand on his shoulder.

"Yeah. Fucker jumped me." Which he could have and had handled. It was hearing him talk about violating Scarlett that nearly caused him to explode. Then turning around and seeing her there? Jesus. He'd lost ten years off his life.

"Those security cameras have fucking paid for themselves twice over now," Jason said as sirens began to sound and cop cars came to a screeching halt inside and outside the alley.

It took a while to sort through the situation, especially with Vic trying to claim he'd been set up, jumped, attacked by Tanner again, among all sorts of other bullshit. The good news was that everything was on tape. Vic had let his hatred of Tanner and the rest of the guys get the best of him, and he'd forgotten about the security cameras. All he'd been focused on was revenge for the years he'd already spent in prison.

Now, thanks to the vandalism he'd caused, the bomb threat he'd called in and admitted to Daniel Sutherland, and the violation of his parole ... the man was going away again for a long, long time.

When the police finally left with Vic, Tanner and the guys headed back inside the bar. They were immediately surrounded by Dares who wanted to know what had happened and if everyone was okay. But Tanner only had eyes for the shaken woman on the barstool in the far corner of the room.

She'd seen him at his worst and he had to wonder how she'd feel about him now. He excused himself from the mass of people and made his way over to her.

She looked up at him with those big green eyes. "You're okay." She touched a hand to what was probably his swollen jaw. It hurt but he'd live.

He nodded. "I'm fine."

She pulled her bottom lip between her teeth. "And Vic?"

"Is with the cops... He's fine too."

She released a long breath. "I knew you wouldn't

hurt him. I believed that you'd keep yourself under control."

He studied her in awe. "Unsure how you knew that when there was a moment I didn't believe it myself."

A smile graced her lips. "Because I know who you are in here." She placed a warm hand over his chest. "*Now* can we go home?"

TANNER KNEW BETTER than to think his battle was over. True, Vic was behind bars, but there was no way he'd go down easily. There'd be a trial and sentencing because Vic was a bastard and if it made their lives more difficult? He'd do everything he could to torture them. Sadistic asshole.

But the next morning, Vic was the last thing on his mind because he knew in his gut Scarlett was going to leave, and if he wanted her forever, he was going to have to let her go first.

She was stubborn, his girl, and right now she was staring at him with those intelligent eyes, and she definitely had something to say.

"What is it?" he asked, looking at her across the bed.

"It's over," she murmured.

He nodded. "It is." Instead of beating around the bush, he went right for the kill. "Can I convince you to stay?"

She blew out a long breath. "It's so fast. We're so new."

He'd expected this. After all, as her father had said, she'd raised herself and was scared of heartbreak. Not to mention she'd lost both her mother and her brother. Fear lived inside her. If he wanted her with him, he needed to be patient. But that didn't mean he'd make it easy.

"I can't just move in with you and assume everything is going to be okay," she said softly.

"Why not?"

She blinked nervously. "Well, we've only been together under stressful circumstances, for one thing. You still don't know that my crazy work schedule and your night one is compatible."

"Faith and Jason make it work."

She opened and closed her mouth. He'd obviously stumped her with that one.

"But if you think we need time, I'll give you time." With more emotional difficulty than he'd ever had before, he rolled out of bed and stood facing her. "Come on. I'll help you get your things together and take them back to your place."

It killed him to do it this way, but she needed to see they could work under ordinary life circumstances. That he was a man who stuck. And that despite what she was telling herself, she really wanted to be here with him. All things she needed to learn for herself. She needed to miss him.

As he'd thought, she was a stubborn woman. But she'd needed to become self-reliant out of necessity. Once he took her home, he hoped she'd realize how very wrong her way of thinking was. Otherwise he was shit out of luck and in a lot of trouble.

✧　✧　✧

SCARLETT HAD BEEN back to her normal routine for one week. Today was the second Monday of *normal*. One week of waking up alone and going to sleep the same way. A week of getting her own lunch and eating by herself. A weekend of working from home, buried in files, but this time Tanner wasn't patiently by her side. And she hated it.

"I just need time to readjust to normal." She said it so often, she was just waiting to believe it.

"Keep telling yourself that," Leigh said from behind her desk.

Instead of Leigh seeking Scarlett out to talk and take a break, it was Scarlett who'd come knocking to see her friend. She'd even taken a walk downstairs and bought Starbucks for them both.

"Tell me again why you left the man you obviously love?"

"I…" She opened and closed her mouth. "I love him."

Leigh narrowed her gaze. "Are you just figuring this out?"

Blowing out a slow breath, Scarlett nodded. "In words, yes. I mean, I never put the words to the feelings."

Leigh steepled her hands and shook her head. "You are really something. For a smart woman, you can be so slow emotionally."

"Hey, it's been hard for me." She could list all the reasons, her background, childhood, history, and none of it mattered. She'd screwed up badly.

"Call him," Leigh said. "Or go see him. But for the love of God, don't lose him."

"I know. I am. I will." She pushed herself up from her seat, gathering the courage as she walked back to her office, where she'd left her cell.

She settled back into her chair, placed her coffee cup on the desk, and picked up her phone to find a text waiting for her.

Are you free for lunch?

Her heart leapt inside her chest at the sight of Tanner's name on the screen. *Yes.*

Sandwich or salad? he asked.

So he was coming here so she could work for as long as possible. Excitement over such a little thing lit her up inside because it showed how well he understood her.

Sandwich, she texted back. *I'm starving.*

She'd skipped breakfast, something she'd been doing because she'd gotten used to having his company over a bowl of cereal or a cup of yogurt in Tanner's kitchen and now she was lonely. Something she didn't want to admit to herself.

Instead of working, she counted the minutes until Tanner stood in her doorway. He cleared his throat. "Did someone order a sandwich?" He held out a plain brown bag.

And God, was he a welcome sight. He wore his faded black jeans and his olive-green Henley. His muscles bulged in the sleeves. She knew he hit the gym after he dropped her off at work. Now he could go whenever he wanted to.

"Come in!" She jumped up and began clearing off her desk, making room for them to eat.

"Relax," he said in that rough voice she adored.

She wondered if he'd waited a week on purpose. So she'd miss him even more. If so, his plan had worked.

He strode over, took the file folders from her hands, and moved the piles over to the windowsill for her. She reached for the bag but he placed it on the desk.

"Forgetting something first?"

She paused, uncertain around him, a feeling she detested. "Umm…"

He held out his arms. "Kiss me, honey."

She blinked, and before she could process the motion, she threw herself against his chest, wrapped her arms around his neck, and sealed her lips over his, thrusting her tongue inside his waiting mouth. He tasted like mint and man, like home and everything good in life.

She stood in the warmth of his embrace and let his kiss wash away the loneliness of the past week and the second-guessing she'd done about leaving him.

"Oh, man. At least shut the door!" Leigh giggled and a second later, the door slammed closed.

Scarlett groaned and buried her head against Tanner's firm chest.

He patted her on the back. "It was just Leigh. You're fine."

She lifted her head and met his gaze. "Want to eat?"

Chuckling, he pulled out her chair for her to ease down into it. They sat across from each other, talking about their past week, discussing the fact that Vic was, in fact, refusing to accept a plea deal, and they were facing a potential trial.

"So I was thinking," Tanner said. "I wanted to lay

out a possible schedule for you and get your opinion."

She wrinkled her nose in confusion. "Okay."

"I asked myself, if I lived with a woman who claimed to work nonstop, when would I see her?"

Her mouth ran dry despite the fact that she was currently sipping from a bottle of water.

"Want to know what I came up with?" He raised his eyebrows.

She managed a nod.

"Well, I'd wake up in the morning with her in my arms. And before work, I'm sure we'd have time for either a quickie in bed or in the shower, or if we woke up earlier, a longer session."

He took a bite of his sandwich as if he were discussing the weather and not their lives. He took his time, chewing and swallowing. "I could take her to work if we wanted to be together then, or she could go by car service. I'd work out at the gym and she'd go to work. You with me so far?"

She nodded again, listening carefully now.

"We could have lunches like these when things are quiet for her and sadly not see each other when she's busy, say in court or with witness prepping." He shrugged. "On days she has to work, she'd go home and do just that. I could have some days with dinner at home, others I'd have to be at the club. So she could meet me there on occasion. And I have partners, so honestly I don't need to be there all the time." Leaning back in his seat, he studied her as he spoke.

"And the weekends?" she whispered, hope lodged in her chest. Although she'd made the choice, it had been the wrong one. Was he offering her a second chance?

"I have nights on and off, alternating with the guys. Sundays we're closed. Monday nights too. I really like sports, and watching television while she works beside me is no hardship."

He finished his sandwich, wrapped up the garbage, hers and his, and tossed it in the trash.

Then he stood. "Thanks for hearing me out. I wanted to say it out loud. Make sure it sounded feasible. I'll just let you get back to work now."

"Wait, what?" She'd barely had time to process what he was saying.

Oh, hell, she knew exactly what he was saying, and she was a complete and utter idiot.

He reached the door, but she was around the desk and turning him toward her before he could open it and expose them to the rest of her office. "Don't go."

He slowly faced her, his expression serious, his gaze staring intently at her.

"I was scared," she admitted to him. "I *am* scared."

His hand stroked gently down her cheek. "Of what? Of me?"

She shook her head. "Of what I feel for you. How I know it can break me if I lose you. I … I know what loss feels like and it's awful."

He braced her face in his hands. "And the last week alone, was it awful?"

She nodded. "The worst. But I told myself it was for the best. I used the walls I built as an excuse to keep from getting close to anyone or getting hurt. But then you barreled into my life and I couldn't find those defenses. I couldn't shore up the walls. You broke down every one. But still, I tried to go back to my regular life because it was safe. And I hated it." Tears filled her eyes and a lump rose in her throat.

All the emotion she hadn't let herself feel came flooding out because last week had been like loss and she never wanted to experience that again.

He brushed at the tears with his thumbs. "I love you, Scarlett. So let me in. Let me be with you in busy times and free times. In good and bad."

She laughed. A real, honest, carefree laugh. "I love you too. And I'm sorry I was an idiot. I should have stayed. I just…"

"You needed to see for yourself what it was like without me or you'd never have understood what we had. You couldn't let yourself believe in it. I get it. I knew before you left that we'd end up right here, right now."

She tipped her head to the side. "How?" How had he been so sure of *them*?

His smile was so sexy it took her breath away. "Because I know you, Scarlett Davis. I know you in here." He placed his hand over her heart, the same way she'd once done to him.

"Now will you get back to work so later on I can take you home, where you belong?"

TANNER SPENT THE afternoon on an errand he'd never pictured himself doing. For shits and giggles, he'd taken Landon along with him since Jason was busy, and he knew his single friend wouldn't understand. Someday, he'd have his elevator moment, as Tanner had come to think of the instant the doors opened and he'd laid eyes on Scarlett. Only then would Jason's and Tanner's lives make sense to their confirmed bachelor partner.

As expected, Landon grunted and groaned through every piece of jewelry they looked at.

"Who gives a shit if it's circular, oval, or square? A diamond's a diamond," he'd said.

Tanner had grinned. "You'll see," was the only answer he had.

Now that he heard the words he'd needed from Scarlett, he was locking shit down. No way was she finding any excuse to leave him again.

He picked her up from work, taking his SUV this time because his nerves demanded that he be in control of something and driving was it. The ring burned a hole in his pocket. Sure, she'd agreed to move in with him, but he knew damn well he was pushing it asking her to marry him so quickly.

He couldn't seem to stop himself. The last week was the most patient he'd ever been. He didn't have another ounce inside him. They'd already gone to her apartment and packed up enough for the rest of the week. This weekend he intended to move everything he could get his hands on into his house.

"Tanner, are you okay?" she asked, touching his arm.

His hand gripped the steering wheel hard. "I'm good. Just going over some things in my head for the event with Tangled Royal."

"I'm so excited for it! Oh! Let's listen to them on CarPlay!" She inserted the plug into her phone, scrolled around, and Lola Corbin's husky voice sounded around them.

The songs calmed him for the duration of the ride, and by the time they walked into the house … he was ready.

He opened the door and Scarlett stepped inside. As per usual, they walked through the kitchen, he dropped his keys in a dish, and they headed upstairs to change. He slid his hand into his pocket, feeling for the ring.

She pushed open the door ... and candles greeted her. Flickering flameless candles because he'd had Felicia, their manager, come by and set up the room. He couldn't risk a real fire.

"Oh my God!" Scarlett stepped inside and he followed. "What is all this?" Scarlett spun around at the same time he lowered himself to one knee.

"Tanner?" Her sweet mouth parted at the sight of him.

He held out the ring he'd tortured Landon to buy, his mouth dry as dirt. "I know I just got you to agree to move back in with me, but I want more. I want it all. With you. Scarlett, will you marry me?"

She didn't even look at the ring. She merely nodded and threw herself against him, something that was becoming a nice habit, knocking him over.

They fell to the floor, her mouth on his, kissing him over and over. He felt around for the ring he'd dropped and pulled his head back. "It's nice to know my fiancée isn't materialistic, but would you like to at least see the ring?"

She grinned and he took in her happiness, feeling it like it was his own. "Sorry. I'm just so happy to be back here with you and I didn't expect a marriage proposal. But since you asked, and I'm not letting you go again ever … yes, and let's see."

He slid the ring onto her finger and she glanced down at the cushion-cut diamond surrounded by a halo of smaller stones. "I love it," she whispered. "And I love you. And your patience. And everything about you. I'm going to make this last week up to you."

He held up her finger wearing his ring and kissed her there. "You already did."

Epilogue

THE BAND TANGLED Royal played on stage at Club TEN29, marking the end of a dark period in Landon's life. One of many. Apparently he was destined to have a shitload of bad stuff dumped on him any time he started to think life could turn itself around. However, Victor Clark was in prison again, this time for what they hoped would be a long fucking time. The club was prospering. And his friends were happy, one married, another engaged. He'd take it.

As he glanced around at the club, which was his life, he thought about his twin. Levi was never far from his mind. Neither was the son his brother never knew he'd had. But Levi's college girlfriend, Amber, was starting a new life too, returning to college this summer and moving closer to Landon and his parents, so they could see ten-year L.J. more often. That was a good thing. He loved L.J. and the notion of being there to help guide him was a good one.

But Landon's focus would always be the club named for the date his twin had died. As he watched

Tangled Royal and thought about how many people a popular live band brought in, an idea began to form: A summer residency at Club TEN29 with a singer people would flock to see.

He could envision it now and he fucking loved it. He'd run it by Jason and Tanner in the morning while they counted receipts from tonight's gig. From there, his thoughts turned to what kind of artist he could find that would check all the boxes.

Dance music.

Talented.

Alluring.

Sexy.

Female.

He'd have his work cut out for him on the search, but it would be so worth the effort when he found her and the money came pouring in.

Can't get enough Sexy? **BETTER THAN SEXY** is up next.

Insta-love only happens in the movies.
Insta-lust? That she'd buy into.
Until she meets take-charge club owner Landon Bennett and falls head over heels at a glance.

When hot as sin Landon Bennet offers sexy songstress Vivienne Clark a summer residency at his popular Manhattan nightclub, it's the opportunity of a lifetime and she can't resist. Add in the man's obvious interest and seductive attention and life is perfect. Until she puts together the pieces of his past. Fate might have brought them together, but is the intimate relationship they've been building strong enough to overcome one painful fact. She's the sister of the man who killed his twin.

GET **BETTER THAN SEXY!**

Want even more Carly books?
CARLY'S BOOKLIST by Series – visit:
http://smarturl.it/CarlyBooklist

Sign up for Carly's Newsletter:
http://smarturl.it/carlynews

Carly on Facebook:
facebook.com/CarlyPhillipsFanPage

Carly on Instagram:
instagram.com/carlyphillips

About the Author

Carly Phillips is the *N.Y. Times* and *USA Today* Bestselling Author of over 50 sexy contemporary romance novels featuring hot men, strong women and the emotionally compelling stories her readers have come to expect and love. Carly's career spans over a decade and a half with various New York publishing houses, and she is now an Indie author who runs her own business and loves every exciting minute of her publishing journey. Carly is happily married to her college sweetheart, the mother of two nearly adult daughters and three crazy dogs (two wheaten terriers and one mutant Havanese) who star on her Facebook Fan Page and website. Carly loves social media and is always around to interact with her readers. You can find out more about Carly at www.carlyphillips.com.

7-6-20
1-10-22
1
0